in the land of glare

stories

laura golden bellotti

ISBN: 978-1-66787-563-7

Angeleno Birch Tree Girl in the Land of Glare

She awakes one October to find a birch tree growing

out of her left shoulder

its sleek white bark barely distinguishable

from her own skin

but placing an embarrassing burden

on her for now

she will have to face the world

as a freak of nature.

She wonders what she has done

to deserve this

and remembers her wish

that she might one day live

where trees flash colors in autumn

instead of the unicolor L.A. dreamscape

where she feels like a foreigner

a shade tree leaf lover in the land of glare

She finds it difficult to walk at first

but soon learns to balance the weight

of the birch tree on her left shoulder

by attracting birds to perch on her right shoulder

in the shadow of her scarlet leaves

the chirping and fluttering of their wings

so familial she doesn't even mind

the blunt stares of undeformed Angelenos.

Contents

It Will Be Sweet

It Will Be Sweet

Batya is jolted awake by the alley cat's frantic cry. She opens an eye and sees her Princess Jasmine digital clock glowing 3:23 a.m., faintly illuminating her sister Hannie's cheek. Hugging her legs to her chest, Batya wonders what's making the cat wail so violently in the middle of the night. She tries to go back to sleep but the yowling won't quit.

Three stray cats make their home in the narrow walkway alongside the Pico-Robertson apartment building where Batya lives with her mother and sister. The cats hunt for bugs in the bushes and curl up on the back stairs on hot or rainy days. Batya and Hannie leave food for them, and the cats seem content with their lazy life. So why this miserable, insistent crying?

Of course Hannie is sleeping through the noise. When the ambulance siren blared into the apartment garage a few weeks ago after someone found the homeless lady collapsed in a pool of motor oil, Hannie slept through the whole thing. Batya thinks about going out to check on the suffering cat, but the meowing suddenly stops.

She closes her eyes again and tries to go back to her dream, remembering only a general feeling—of anticipation and danger—and the bristling sound of the wind. Batya can hear the neighbor's wind chimes now, but the tinkling is faint so there must be only a slight breeze, not the menacing wind of her dream. Last week when the Santa Anas started up, the Israeli guy across the way who calls his wife a stupid bitch knocked on the wind chime owners' door and yelled at them to take it down—but Batya likes hearing the clinking strips of glass.

Now the cry is back, its voice more pitiful, as if the cat could be on the brink of crying human tears. Batya sits up and feels in the dark for her sweatshirt at the foot of the bed. The "aoow, aoow" grows louder as she slips the shirt over her head and gets up to check on her adopted pet. What could be causing it such distress?

But then she realizes…

It's not a cat.

The catch in its voice, the half-laugh, the whimper that Batya feels in her own chest, tell her that it's a woman.

Batya has never heard this sound before. She knows what it is, but at the same time she doesn't know. Blurry shapes of a naked woman and man coming together flare in her mind. But imagining them makes her ashamed. Against her will, she is drawn into their room, embarrassed by the tingling between her legs. As if the woman's shattered voice is penetrating her own body. Batya forces herself to let out the shallow breath trapped in her lungs.

At fourteen, Batya has no experience with boys. She is unsure of exactly what they do to make a girl cry out like this. Her mother has given her only generalizations. It will be sweet when you are with the right man and you are married, Bati, she has said. Until then, enjoy your childhood—and pay attention to your studies. Her mother mentioned nothing about a woman crying out in the middle of the night like a wounded animal. And Batya has heard nothing about this from her teachers or the girls at her Jewish school.

Batya has become more religious since moving to the U.S. Living in Israel she was Jewish without thinking about it. Here, you have to stick to your own kind or you'll be swallowed up by all the other races and religions. Like the Persian Jewish guy with his high-heeled Japanese girlfriend. That's why Batya's mother insisted she and Hannie go to an Orthodox school instead of a public one.

The cries are coming in jabs of sound now. Closer together, with more in-taking of breath. Batya pulls the pillow over her head and closes her eyes, but she can still hear. "Aoow, aoow!"—and then "aah, aah!"

She gets up and goes to the half-opened window overlooking the walkway and tries to pinpoint where the cries are coming from. Whose apartment? The "aah, aah"—sometimes a breathy "huh, huh"—echoes in the space between her building and the one next door so that Batya can't determine where it starts. She listens to the voice and rolls through the possibilities in her mind.

It could be coming from the Persian guy's apartment down-stairs. Batya has noticed that every weekend after Shabbat, he brings home that tall, thin Japanese woman with sparkling green eye shadow. She could easily be the voice. Her high heels and tight skirts say that crying out like this with a boy you're not going to marry is perfectly fine. In fact, it's something you desperately want—and even tell your girlfriends about afterward. The Persian guy graduated from UCLA and sells real estate. He's as handsome as an American movie star and wears silky grey suits for Shabbat. The way he saunters to his silver sports car, his long legs agile and deliberate, makes Batya think of a panther. He never notices her even when she's walking in his direction. Batya has stared at the Japanese woman's outlined red lips and made-up eyes and tried to imagine what she might have looked like at Batya's age.

Now the cries are more like moans, almost like when Hannie, who's three years younger than Batya, tries to get their mother to give in, to let her have something that's not good for her—like candy or a second piece of cake.

Riveted by the high-pitched moaning, Batya has the uncomfortable sense that the voice could be T.J.'s mother. T.J. and his parents live upstairs in the front of the building and the sound would have to travel two apartments down, but his parents' bedroom faces onto the walkway, so it's possible. Batya has seen T.J.'s parents kiss in public, like other grown-ups born in this country. Would his mother dare to make noises like this—with T.J. sleeping in the next room? Before Batya's father died and their family still lived in Netanya, her parents' bedroom was close to her's and Hannie's. But she was too young then to think about her parents making love. Now, Batya tries to erase the mental image of T.J.'s mother's face uttering such fierce sounds.

The moaning stops and all Batya hears is the distant whoosh of a bus speeding down Pico Boulevard. How lonely to be a bus driver in the middle of the night when everyone's asleep.

The "aah, aah!" sound is back, louder and more pleading. Batya wonders if it could be the red-haired lady rabbi next door. She and her too-friendly husband are reform Jews in their twenties. The rabbi mostly wears jeans, and her husband always stops to chat with Batya and Hannie, asks how they're doing in school, what they're learning in Torah class. Batya doesn't like the rabbi's husband. Maybe it's the way his rude eyes dart down to Batya's breasts, which embarrass her because they've grown so large, or maybe it's the wiry black chest hair poking out of his tank top. He makes her cringe. She doesn't want to, but now she can't help picturing him rocking up and down on top of his wife, pawing her breasts and making her scream like this. But the rabbi seems too shy to cry out so publicly.

The woman's voice has grown softer, the "oh, oh" more tender—almost like the soothing tone Batya's mom uses when she comforts Batya or Hannie. What is the man doing to the woman now to make her cries more gentle? And why can't Batya hear the man's voice? Maybe men are supposed to stay silent through the whole thing. And maybe women are the ones who lose control. Batya again feels a wave of sensation between her legs, which shames and baffles her. She doesn't understand why her body should respond to what's happening in a neighbor's bedroom. It has nothing to do with her.

She tries again to identify the voice. She knows it can't be that of the sad-eyed Israeli woman directly across the walkway, the wife of the guy who hates the wind chimes. Batya feels sorry for her. She has heard the husband yelling at his wife in Hebrew, calling her an idiot so the whole neighborhood hears. He could never be gentle to anyone. Batya is sure the two of them hate each other too much to ever kiss or have sex. She has noticed how the woman puts all her love into her tiny garden on the edge of the walkway. Planting, watering, trimming. Batya has even heard her talking to the mint and fennel plants. *How are you today, my sweet ones, growing so fast!* If Batya were married to such a horrible husband, she'd go crazy and talk to the herbs too.

An "Oh, oh! No, no!" pierces the almost silent night.

Batya gets back into bed. The voice is deeper now, as if it's coming from the woman's chest, not her mouth. Batya can't picture such a gruff, raw sound coming out of her own mouth. It's barely human. And what do the crude noises have to do with love? With the queasy feeling Batya gets when she walks home from shul with Aaron?

She is embarrassed to be thinking of Aaron now as she listens to the woman's cries becoming more ferocious, more insistent.

She sticks her fingers in her ears and tries not to listen, but still hears. After shul on Saturday, Batya and Aaron walked together for a few blocks on the way to his family's apartment for lunch. Aaron is two years older and someone Batya would love to kiss. His lips are full and serious. His eyes intensely study her face, instead of darting around at whoever else is passing by, like most boys'. During lunch she felt his eyes on her, and she couldn't eat. She loved the fluttering feeling of being looked at as a woman instead of a girl.

The crying out escalates into a near scream. Batya can't believe that the howling woman doesn't feel utterly humiliated. Is this the first time this has happened, or just the first time Batya has heard it? How could she not have heard such wild, embarrassing screams before?

A neighbor yells out, *Keep it down*! and Hannie turns over in her bed, moaning in her sleep.

Batya looks at the clock. It's 3:48. How long does sex last? Another question she could never ask her mother. The screams get louder, more rhythmic and unrelenting—like the shameless neighborhood crows that caw back and forth from one stretch of phone wires to another. Someone bangs a window shut.

Then the screams turn into one long pleading moan—aaaaaaaaaah!

And it's over.

The only sound left in the walkway is that of the fallen ficus leaves, blowing down the pavement as a faint wind picks up.

Batya is aware that her heart is pounding and that her hand has slipped between her legs. She leaves it there, then looks over at

Hannie tossing in her sleep and quickly moves her hand away. She hears her own breath, like a silent version of the unknown neighbor's cries. How long before she will go through the same thing? Some girls her age are already having sex, girls who go to public school and let their belly buttons show, like the models on MTV. Batya's mother doesn't like her to watch MTV, but she does sometimes when her mom is at work. Girls not much older than Batya are almost having sex right there in the videos, their hips and breasts shaking, their glossy lips parted as if they're crying out like Batya's neighbor.

But Batya has to wait until she's married. Orthodox girls must wait, but they're encouraged to get married young—and have babies right away to fulfill God's wishes.

What do a woman's cries have to do with God? Is it what He wants women to feel? Batya listens to the plinking of the wind chimes and finally falls back to sleep.

At 7:02 Batya startles awake with the droning noise of the leaf blower. Closing her eyes again, she is aware of other sounds beneath the leaf blower's whirring. The blender in the kitchen, where her mother is making a smoothie for Hannie; the Pico buses; the helicopters that report on the traffic; the crows cawing; her alarm clock. She turns it off and goes to the window overlooking the walkway.

Maybe the voice was just a dream. Maybe it really was a cat and Batya's dreaming self made up the rest. She watches the gardener blowing a handful of leaves down the walkway with his heavy machine. It's strapped on his back while he points the hose-like blower at the stray leaves. All the gardeners in Pico-Robertson are from Mexico, and Batya wonders if they're glad to be living in L.A. Or do they miss their home, like she misses Netanya. In Netanya, she was still a little girl, the sweet pleasures in her life unquestioned and uncomplicated.

Batya turns from the window and puts on her bathrobe. When the leaf blower turns off his machine, she hears the Israeli guy yell at his wife in Hebrew as he heads down the walkway to work. *Idiot! Get the hell inside and put on some clothes!* Batya is about to go into the kitchen when she thinks she hears the voice from last night. At the window she listens for it amid the morning noises.

She's not sure. First she hears the clicking of high heels, then the high-pitched laughter of the Japanese girlfriend. The laugh is in the same range as the cries from last night. The girl yells *Ciao!* and blows a kiss through the Persian guy's window. Then Batya notices the Israeli's wife kneeling by her garden in her nightgown. She's weeping as she waters the mint, her cries barely distinguishable from the brazen girl's laugh.

The cry or the laugh—which is it? Which got tangled up in her own body so that she can't forget? Batya listens for another moment, then leaves her bedroom window and goes to bring breakfast to the homeless cats.

Empathy

Empathy

Jamie was in his mother's arms when she was shot to death. The bullet, intended for the guy standing beside her, missed its mark and killed Yolanda instantly. The incident was not uncommon in Yolanda's neighborhood. What was remarkable was that her month-old son was unharmed. Placed in the custody of his grandmother, Jamie was well cared for in the weeks to follow. But his health would progressively deteriorate.

*

Geoff assumed it was the baby's ordeal that triggered Claire's decline. He should have known. Claire's beauty was witch-scary, her spirit too intense, her composure too easily shattered.

*

Jamie refused to eat. He cried incessantly and failed to respond to his grandmother's attempts to soothe him. Hours would pass and the baby's rabid cries would not abate. His grandmother tried everything: holding, rocking, singing. A social worker told her about the bundling technique: *Wrap up the baby tightly in his blankets so that he feels as secure as he did in the womb.* The grandmother followed the social worker's suggestion, learning exactly how to fold the blankets so that the infant resembled a papoose. It didn't work. The crying persisted and Jamie continued to refuse a bottle. A neighbor told the grandmother to run the vacuum cleaner. The white noise would calm the baby, the neighbor said, because it would remind him of the womb's fluid swishing sounds. The grandmother tried it but Jamie's cries became more tormented.

*

As a child, Claire instinctively felt the emotional pain of others and was compelled to alleviate it. In elementary school, she took it upon herself to befriend the outcasts who suffered ongoing taunts and humiliations. Although her beauty and un-showy intelligence would have assured her a position on the highest rung of popularity, she pulled away from the well-liked cliques and watched out for the sad ones: the fat girls who everyone else snickered at, the pointy-headed boys who were too goofy smart and awkward to avoid ridicule.

She felt it was her responsibility to quietly prove to these undesir-ables that they were understood and loved. At lunch Claire sat with Penelope Gross, whose very name drew sneers and whose hunched posture and potato shape made her look prematurely aged. Claire graciously traded her Oreos for Penelope's soggy graham crackers and told Penelope she liked her new brown glasses. Because she could feel his despair as if it were her own, Claire chose Arthur Blanger (another unattractively named pariah) for her third-grade dodge-ball team. *So what if we get hit by the ball?* Claire reassured the toothpick-bodied Arthur, whose homely face broadcast his panic as the ball was about to be hurled by an ace-shot on the other team. *It only hurts for a second*, she promised.

*

The grandmother had little time to grieve for her murdered daughter. Her energy was spent trying to care for her distressed infant grandson, who was now losing weight due to his inability to take the bottle. She cuddled and sang to him as she tried to ease the rubber nipple between his lips, but he would shake his head from side to side and his crying would increase. *I am your mommy now,* she would whisper, *the only mommy you've got.* But the baby boy couldn't hear her over his own wails.

*

In college, the first in a string of lovers accused Claire of being too nice: *Your sweetness makes you dull. You have no edge. You need to expose yourself to the world and get kicked around.* Claire took the boyfriend's criticism to heart and resolved to put herself into situations where she could experience the hardships that would enlighten and strengthen her. She took a year off from her college studies and joined AmeriCorps, accepting a tutoring position in a gang-infested neighborhood. On her way to a student's home one evening, she was accosted by a group of toughs from the high school. *Hey teacher! Sexy fox!* they taunted. One of the teenagers grabbed at her breasts and crotch as the others stood by and laughed. As she firmly broke away, Claire saw in the young man's eyes abandonment and terror, and she felt in her own bones how lost he was. He can't help it, she told herself. His family is broken.

*

Claire appreciated her mother's exuberance and daring but knew Madeline was not like other moms. During Claire's junior year of college, Madeline left Claire's father to test the waters of independence, flirting with men in high class clubs and hoping to get something going. Claire understood why her mother needed to break free from her loyal yet dull father. She also felt her mother's self-loathing beneath the cheerful, make-up sweetened face that struggled to attract an exciting lover. Madeline never found the man she was looking for and returned to her demoralized husband who took her back, no questions asked. Empathizing with her mother's failed quest for the passionate life, Claire also felt the deepening sadness of her well-meaning father who would never elicit passion in anyone.

Her parents' off-kilter relationship and her own ambivalent response to it drove Claire to become a psychologist. ·

*

On the fourth day after the murder, Jamie was so weak he stopped crying. He was still refusing nourishment and had lost two pounds. When the social worker came by and discovered the severity of the infant's condition, she ordered the grandmother to go to the E.R.

*

Claire decided to focus her psychology practice on survivors of child abuse after hearing a friend's story of being sexually abused by an uncle. Adults who struggled with the after-effects of having been sexually, physically, or emotionally abused by a father, stepfather, teacher, or even a mother, recounted the years of being unable to trust or have normal sexual relationships—and worked with Claire to regain those abilities. Then there were the children, many of whom could not use words to describe what had happened to them. So Claire offered crayons and paper, dolls and other toys to allow the younger ones to tell their story.

When friends asked Claire about her practice, she would respond only in generalities. The horror of what her patients had been through was too painful for Claire to describe. She was a powerful advocate for her clients, who experienced her as the strong protector they had lacked during childhood. She was caring yet professional during therapeutic sessions. But outside her office, she was haunted by the cruelty and degradation her clients had suffered. Injuries inflicted by a parent's beating, vaginal and anal tissue torn by a brutal rape—Claire felt the pain in her own body. Eating dinner alone in her apartment after a long day of treating her patients, she couldn't think about a particular client's story without feeling as if it were happening to her. Tears of rage and sorrow would mount and she would switch on a TV program or open a novel to try to escape.

*

The baby improved slightly with intravenous feeding, but it was a protocol that could not be undertaken indefinitely. The doctors informed Jamie's grandmother that they knew of no physical reason why the baby couldn't eat. The grandmother wondered if she would soon be burying another piece of herself.

*

Claire heard stories of fathers raping daughters as young as six years old and imprisoning them in a web of lies throughout their childhood; of young boys being sodomized by an uncle or family friend and threatened with worse if they told; of women so confused and traumatized by what had happened to them that some had turned to prostitution, others to a cautious, sexless existence. The simple act of listening was balm for the victims' emotional wounds. As Claire validated their sometimes buried feelings, her clients became open to the possibility of healing the scars of betrayal. But the stories became embedded in Claire's psyche after she left the office: during workouts at the gym, when she was oblivious to the guys trying to chat her up; at dinner with friends, who noticed she was never fully present.

Since the first day she began her work with abuse victims, Claire was aware of the fact that she could not separate herself from the lives of those she was helping. She could not erect a sturdy boundary between herself and the horrors her clients recounted. Gradually she began to feel the abuse in her own body. The punching and bruising of flesh; the marks left by rough insistent hands pressing over her mouth to suppress a scream; genital tissue violated and scraped raw; and worst of all, the ongoing fear that a trusted human being could turn into a monster in a heartbeat.

Claire's gift—and curse—was her ability to suffer in her very cells what her clients had suffered, so that they could purge the terror from their minds and bodies, giving it up to their all-caring therapist.

*

More than a week after the shooting, the baby's father, Alonso, came to see his son in the hospital. He had attended Yolanda's memorial service and told Yolie's mother he would be by to see the baby, but this was the first time he had made it. Jamie was no longer crying but still wasn't eating and was getting weaker.

Your boy may not survive, the grandmother told Alonso. *He'll make it*, Alonso said, stroking Jamie's face with the back of his hand. *He's a fighter like me.*

*

I met someone in the bakery who would be perfect for you, Madeline told her daughter. *I just have this feeling...*

The bakery? Claire took deep breaths as she struggled to recover from today's session: a twelve-year-old client raped by her grandfather as he pressed a huge fat hand over her mouth.

We started chatting while I waited for my Danish. He does something with computers but seems real sensitive. And he's gorgeous. Tall, single, thirty-something.

Claire rarely dated. After too many confusing sexual encounters she was trying to keep her personal life uncomplicated. She had too easily fallen, not in love but under a kind of spell that she found disorienting. If she had been able to engage in casual sex, she could have avoided the sense of losing herself whenever she became involved with a lover. But there was nothing casual about Claire. And after working with her troubled clients, she craved solitude at the end of her long day.

What makes you think he's sensitive?

He bought me two black-and-white cookies and told me to give one to you.

Sweet... And how did he know about me, Mom?

Claire didn't have to ask, knowing that her mother loved to brag about her. She had a clear mental image of her mom reaching for the photo in her wallet as she told the stranger about her brilliant psychologist daughter.

I showed him your picture and gave him your number.

Claire didn't have it in her to disappoint her mother. She wanted to quell the fears Madeline had about her not being normal, and she knew her mom would relax a little if a boyfriend were on the horizon.

Thanks, Mom…I'll look forward to hearing from your cookie guy.

*

The doctors could not send the baby home until he was able to take a bottle, and that was still not happening. Every day the grandmother sat by his hospital crib, expecting the worst but praying for a miracle. She watched as the nurses attempted to feed Jamie, only to see him listlessly turn his tiny head away. Why was this little one so stubborn? Didn't he want to live? Didn't God want him to grow up and fill the space in her heart that Yolie had left? The grandmother held the special rosary beads that had belonged to her mother, but for the first time in her life she had little faith in their power.

*

Claire liked the sound of Geoff's voice on the phone and agreed to meet him for dinner.

How'd you like the cookie?—his first words when they met outside the Indian restaurant. She liked him immediately and could tell that he was attracted to her. Unfortunately, he was too attractive. She would have to hold herself in check. It had been months since she had slept with anyone and she already knew she wanted him. During dinner there had been the obligatory questions about each other's careers, and he looked at her with concern when she gave him the abbreviated version of her work with survivors of child abuse.

How do you handle all that pain?

Sometimes I can't.

*

I know of someone who may be able to help. The social worker had
visited Jamie's grandmother several times over the course of the
child's hospital stay, informing her of various resources that would
be available to her when she brought the baby home. But until now
she had not offered the grandmother any advice on dealing with the
crisis of the baby not eating.

*There is a psychologist who comes highly recommended. She would be
open to meeting your grandson.*

The grandmother thought the suggestion strange and inappropriate,
and she was suspicious of the social worker's intent.

*I don't need to talk to anyone. I don't have a problem. The only problem
is my baby won't eat.*

The grandmother suspected that this woman with the stylish hair
and expensive jewelry was trying to get the goods on her, trying to
take her grandson away from her. She would not allow it. Yolanda's
baby was hers now. A psychologist would twist the truth, ask questions she wouldn't be able to answer, and make it seem like she would
not be a good guardian for Jamie.

No, I don't want to see a psychologist.

The baby would be her patient, Mrs. Guerrero, not you

*

Claire fooled herself. *I can do this*. *I can have a relationship like
a normal thirty-four-year-old woman.* Over the years whenever she
had tried to have a night out with friends, she couldn't stop mentally
replaying one scene or another from the week's disturbing case his-
tories. It was as if it was her ongoing duty to never let go of her cli-
ent-victims, to keep them uppermost in her consciousness regardless

of the social gathering she was peripherally engaged in. After all, how important were drinks after work or a colleague's birthday party compared to the rape of a first grader? If she let the survivor slip her mind, what did that say about her priorities?

*

The grandmother was so focused on Jamie that Yolanda's absence had not sunk in. Maybe she couldn't think about her daughter because the pain was too great. Maybe she had to avoid her grief in order to be strong for the baby. If an image of Yolie broke through while she sat watching over her grandson, she pushed it away. Yolie riding her tricycle in the rain. Yolie spinning her globe, asking, *which country is this one, mommy?* Yolie heading outside on that last Saturday afternoon, her new baby in her arms. Glimpses of her daughter were too sweet and too brief to bear. The infant boy was where her attention must remain. She had finally agreed to the crazy idea of a psychologist after the doctor told her they were running out of options.

I know it doesn't make much sense for a psychologist to treat your grandson, Mrs. Guerrero, but Jamie isn't taking a bottle and he can't stay on I.V. forever.

So she gave her okay. But who ever heard of a baby needing a psychologist? Yolanda's boy was not crazy.

*

Claire had never treated a baby. The youngest client she had ever seen was three years old. His mother had beaten him so badly that his eye was swollen shut and two baby teeth were knocked out. It had taken her a number of sessions to gain the boy's trust and begin the slow process of helping him understand that not every adult was someone to be feared. But a five-week-old infant? How would she approach him, communicate with him?

The baby's file contained medical reports on his condition since the day of the shooting, as well as the police report, which included photographs of the crime scene. The seventeen-year-old mother had been standing on her front lawn near the sidewalk with the baby in her arms, talking to a male neighbor. A car drove past, slowed down, and a male passenger shot at the neighbor, missing him but hitting the baby's mother on the left side of the chest. Upon the bullet's impact, the mother fell to the grass, the baby still in her arms. The child, having been held on the right side of the mother's chest, was not hit. The neighbor fled and the baby's grandmother ran outside, grabbed the screaming baby and called 911. The mother was pronounced dead at the scene. The photographs showed her lying on the grass in her jeans and bloody sweatshirt. Her arm was still positioned as if holding the baby. The grandmother stood off to the side, the crying child in her arms.

Claire would meet the baby in the morning.

That evening she mentioned the case to Geoff on the phone after they'd made plans to get together that weekend.

Poor little guy. He needs someone like you on his side.

Can you imagine what it would be like to be in the arms of your mother as she is shot to death?

I don't think an infant is aware of all that. He probably was startled in the moment, but a baby isn't aware of what a gunshot is.

Right. But he's aware of what his mother is.

*

Claire stood outside the hospital room trying to compose herself. Reviewing the report, she heard the gunshot: thundering and abrasive, shattering the baby – the bereft baby in the hospital and herself as a baby – both of them going deaf from the awful blast. She experienced the mother falling, crashing to the ground, the single shot obliterating the baby's world. Claire felt the bullet entering her own chest, her arms loosening their hold on the phantom infant.

Claire had to hold herself together now. Meeting the grandmother and the infant for the first time, she would be calm. She would learn from the baby what he needed from her.

*

The grandmother was not expecting someone who looked like Claire. Tall and beautiful, like a strange goddess from another world. Wild blond hair that hung past her shoulders. A cape for a jacket and sandals like in the bible days. But the woman looked her directly in the eye when the social worker introduced them.

I'm Claire. I'm so sorry about your daughter.

The grandmother could tell she meant it.

May I hold Jamie?

*

Claire took off her cape and lifted the baby out of his hospital crib. He whimpered softly, lacking the energy to cry. She had not held many babies in her life, but after adjusting her arms to accommodate his tiny body, she felt comfortable. He continued to whine in his weak voice. She looked into his eyes, brown and pale, letting him know she wanted to understand him. Careful not to create a jarring motion, she swayed slowly from side to side and continued looking into his eyes. The boy in her arms weighed so little that the substance of her own body seemed massive. Was it a human that she held or some small, helpless animal? She listened to his half-cries, waiting for the clue to his misery. Blocking out the others in the room, she closed her eyes and tuned in fully to the person in her arms. The sounds he emitted were of a deep distress emanating from a place shared by every human regardless of age. He was trying to communicate in the only way he could his wordless protest: anger... fear... despair...grief.

*

The psychologist visited her grandson three times. Twice in the hospital, once at home. During the first visit the woman said nothing, just held the baby and swayed from side to side so that her body became a cradle. On the second visit, she did the same thing but talked to the baby as if he could understand her.

Oh, Jamie. I am so sorry. I'm so sorry, Jamie. So very sorry.

Over and over she spoke to him in a quiet voice as she walked slowly around the room with him in her arms.

The baby started to take the bottle after the woman's second visit, and the grandmother wondered if the psychologist was some kind of *curandera*. She had broken the spell. Yolanda's child was recovering. He would survive.

On the third visit, when the psychologist came to the grandmother's house, she did not look well. She held the baby and talked sweetly to him, but she seemed frail and tired. Her long bushy blonde hair was losing its color.

*

It was a simple discovery: the baby needed to grieve and no one had realized that until Claire held him and listened. She knew as soon as she heard his weak, insistent moaning. Everyone who had dealt with him—the police officials, doctors, nurses, child welfare workers, and even his grandmother—had assumed he could be handed over to a loving substitute mother and that would be enough. They had neglected to factor in the child's irreplaceable loss. He had suffered more than the trauma of a violent incident. He had lost his mother, and as young as he was, the baby needed to mourn that loss.

At first, Claire had just listened to the child, respecting the sounds he made as his only means of communicating. Then, with the tone of her voice and her few words, she let the baby know that she was deeply sorry for his loss, that she understood his intense sorrow and suffering. *I'm so sorry, Jamie. How horrible this loss is for you. Your dear mother taken from you. I'm so sorry, dear boy.*

Although he didn't understand the words, he understood the feeling behind them. Offering the same sincere emotion she would give to anyone who had lost a loved one, Claire conveyed her heartfelt condolences, but she also let Jamie know that she acknowledged his unique agony. His mother had been shot and he had witnessed it, but he was unable to speak or to understand his own confusion and terror. He was devastated by the loss of the most important – the only important – person in his life. In an instant his world had been shattered.

*

Claire's ability to experience what the baby was feeling, and to let him know that, allowed the child to release some of his pain and begin to heal.

But now, having given Jamie the comfort that would save him, Claire had fully absorbed his grief. This time the transfer of her client's agony was complete. She could not release the infant's anguish from her own terrorized body.

*

Geoff hadn't heard from Claire since the night before her first hospital visit with the baby. She had called him to cancel their date. A week or so later, on the night of her last visit to the infant boy, Claire knocked on Geoff's door. *I need you.*

They didn't talk. He offered her some wine and then they made love. It was frantic, violent. Claire pounded him with her body. Sobbing. Pounding. Beating her fists against his body. Crying out like a wounded animal.

She left in the middle of the night.

*

I never knew the whole story. I knew my mom died holding me when I was a baby and that she was shot by some gang banger even though the bullet wasn't meant for her. She was only seventeen. My grandma told me that my mom wanted to travel the world. And she was a good student, liked math like I do. I don't know if she was into art at all, but if she were alive I could tell her that I'm getting an internship at a graphic design company after I graduate. She'd probably think that was cool.

My grandma and I were talking about my mom and how she would be proud of me, and I said wasn't it kind of a miracle that I wasn't killed when she was. And she said, yes, it was a miracle but there was another miracle she couldn't tell me about before. She didn't want to burden me with another sad story, she said, because my mom dying was enough for any kid to handle. But now that I'm old enough...

And then she told me about the lady who came to the hospital when I was a baby and whispered to me when I wouldn't eat. She walked around with me and whispered to me, and I'm not sure why it saved me, but my grandma says it did. My grandma said the lady died a few days after I got better, and that her death was a big shock. There was nothing physically wrong with her. She just died.

It's too bad my mom isn't around to go to my graduation, but my grandma says she'll be there in spirit. It's also too bad that lady had to die so young because now I'll never be able to tell her thanks—for everything.

Blood Mother

Blood Mother

September 20

I like the strict procedures at the LAPD. You know where you stand and what's expected of you. No B.S. Last month I joined the Explorers because I found out they train you for LAPD. Teach you all the protocols and then when you apply to the force you're given special consideration. Even now we get to do cool stuff. Like guard duty at special events. I pulled duty at the Academy Awards a few weeks ago, and then today I worked an event at Fox Hills Mall for the ex-President who was campaigning for some woman running for mayor. When I'm on duty I feel like more than just a nobody. I'm someone who's doing something with his life. Like if I didn't show up, harm could come to people I don't even know, even someone like the President. Tonight I started thinking about all the things I'll get to do after I join the force, and I got really charged. It was like seeing a movie I'm in that hasn't come out yet. Like one of those previews where all the dramatic parts pop out at you hyper fast so you already know the most exciting things that are going to happen.

September 21

Today's my seventeenth birthday, which you probably remember. I bought this notebook to write down what happens to me this year so I can give it to you a year from now. I figure once I find your address I can send it to you before you meet me so you'll have a preview.

I've been looking at your photo all my life, but now I can finally see myself in your face. And even your handwriting is like mine where you signed it *To my precious son from his mother who will never stop loving him.* Even though my mom's the one who raised me since I was two days old, she'll never be my blood mother. Maybe that's why she has such a hard time seeing things my way. Like why I want to join the force. Not classy enough for her. I know *you* would back me up all the way. I can tell by what you wrote on your photo that you believe in me because I'm your son. My mom told me that next year when I turn eighteen I'll be able to look you up. If I can find you, I know I'll finally have someone on my side.

September 27

Except for my sister who thinks L.A. cops are retarded, girls seem to like the uniform and the whole deal of being unofficially part of LAPD. Like this girl I met night before last while I was on duty at a rock concert. She kept making eye contact with me while she was standing there with her friend who came outside to smoke. All I had to say was *How're you doing?* and she started asking me how long I'd been a security officer and did I ever have to apprehend anybody and what did I do for fun. So I got her number and went out with her tonight. When I picked her up she wanted me to meet her mother because she told her I look like a Latino Johnny Depp and that she'd never known anyone as polite as me. Of course she turned out to have loose morals like most of the girls in this city. She was all over me in the movies and all I did to provoke it was hold her hand.

October 10

It's obvious that my sister Sarah has no interest in what it's like to be an Explorer. Tonight I was explaining to her how strenuous the physical fitness training is and how I had come in second at our training session, and she just shot back with *Wow, Mr. Tough Guy Cop's gonna scare away all the criminals.* She's so into her little world of snobby Jewish high school that she doesn't even know there's life on the planet outside of Pico-Robertson. Did the agency tell you that my sister was born when I was only a year old? I guess you lost touch with them after you gave me to them. Anyway, it's pretty funny because, as you obviously know, my parents adopted me thinking they couldn't have a kid of their own. And then a year later, they had her. So Sarah is the blonde angel—well, actually the blonde bitch. She's nasty to me ten days outta nine. But my parents don't see it. They think Sarah is perfect. Straight A's. Popular. Nice Jewish girl if you don't mind fakers. When Sarah and I were little I guess we liked each other. I have this photo of us at the beach bouncing a big red ball, and we're laughing pretty hard so I guess we were happy back then.

October 24

So my sister is going off to the holy land—whoopee. Good for her and I hope she has fun teasing all those Israeli dickheads. I guess you wanted me to be adopted by a Jewish family because my mom told me she got me through a Jewish agency. But did you know I'd end up in this crazy neighborhood? Persian Jews who listen to belly dancing music, sexy Orthodox girls in their ridiculous long skirts, and rabbis snooping around restaurants to make sure it's kosher enough? It's kind of a joke that I'm Jewish. I mean, I know you aren't—my parents told me that you're part Mexican and part Hawaiian. And even though my mom is Jewish, she only goes through the motions for Sarah. My dad was raised Baptist and only converted for my mom's sake. He could care less what's in all the Hebrew prayers that he doesn't understand but lip syncs to when we go to services. As long as he thinks he's doing his bit to build our character he's happy with himself. But Pico-Robertson is where all the Orthodox live, so he and my mom try to blend in and Sarah loves being the beautiful religious girl with the bouncy laugh and killer Hebrew accent. So this afternoon she comes home all excited about taking off for Israel next summer. Her little group of friends are all going, and I guess she figures she'll meet some hot Israeli commando or something. No way I'd ever want to go there, especially now. If I wanted to get killed I could think of better ways to go.

November 7

All the talk about Sarah's big travel plans is getting really old so I had dinner at Benny's again tonight. He's three years younger than me, kind of like my little brother in a way, and lives two apartments down. I eat dinner with his family a lot, almost like I'm their second son. My mom works the graveyard shift captioning films for deaf people, so she's never around to make dinner anyway, and my dad, the dedicated househusband who can't tear himself away from Turner classic movies, mostly makes tacos or brings in crappy take-out. So tonight I'm at Benny's and his mom asks me what it was like to see the President, who I think she has a big crush on, and I tell her how friendly he was to everybody, including me, and she's beaming at me like she's really proud of me. Of course Benny blurts out that I'm exaggerating big time and that the President didn't come anywhere near where I was standing guard. But it's almost like Benny's mom sees me as better than I really am. Like even if she knew I was lying, she would still be proud of me. The way she looks at me is how I imagine you would if you got the chance to be around me.

December 15

My mom made us all trek off today to this little fake Danish village near Santa Barbara on what she called a quote unquote family outing. We were in the car driving up the coast, Sarah was hating on me about my C minus average, and my mom cuts in with *We rarely get the chance to be together as a family—think you two can handle it?* So we tried. We stuffed ourselves with Danish pancakes and butter cookies, and then while my mom bought magnets in the shape of windmills and my dad sat on a bench plugged into his gay Beach Boys CD, Sarah and I had a little brother - sister chat. She told me I should think about Santa Monica City College because they even let people like me in. And I told her she should watch out for those Israeli studs because she wouldn't want to get herself pregnant even with a kosher baby. Then my mom posed us in front of this giant pretzel and snapped one for the family album. I suppose this was a big deal vacation for us since we usually don't take trips—especially now that my parents are saving up for Sarah's holy trek. Her "birthright" as they call it here in P-Ro. Returning to the motherland: Woo ha! My parents obviously think that's a hell of a lot more earth-shattering than joining the force.

January 17

One of the people who's nicest to me other than Benny's mom is an old rabbi at the Jewish day school I got kicked out of—Rabbi Feinman. He's a funny guy who used to get me out of class once in a while to fix the computers cuz he knows I'm good at that stuff. I stopped in to see him today and like he always does he told some of his famous jokes. He always tries to make me laugh. Even though they aren't my kind of jokes and I've heard them a zillion times, I laughed anyway—to make him feel good. Sometimes I imagine you laughing. Your smile in the photo is so sweet. But I wonder what would make you laugh out loud. What kind of jokes you like. I know it wouldn't be the nasty kind of jokes the whores at school tell. My parents don't seem to get that this low life public high school they put me in actually expects you to act like a gangster.

February 20

I didn't mean to get Benny in trouble. It's just that we used his computer so the police came to his apartment today instead of mine. Okay, so I wasn't supposed to bring the police radios home from Explorers, but I was going to return them. Even Benny's dad was impressed when I showed him how we could listen in on all the crimes that were happening in the neighborhood. Then I just thought it'd be cool to see what we could get for one on e-Bay. I wasn't actually planning to sell them. I was just curious. And man, people were willing to pay a lot, really a lot. Only now with this whole code orange security alert and everything, the police figure I'm some kind of teenage terrorist. So they took me down to West L.A. Division and booked me on stealing police equipment and attempting to traffic in stolen goods. This is really going to hurt my chances of getting into LAPD.

March 5

It's definite now. I'm getting kicked out of Explorers for the whole police radio thing. I pulled up to the meeting tonight and my commander ushered me into this sweaty little room. Tells me I'm not Explorer material, that what I did was a serious crime. And here I thought this guy was on my side—all those weeks telling me he believed in me, that the Explorers were like a family. Anyway, forget the LAPD. I don't have a chance. Even if I manage to get this erased from my record, it'll show up if I ever wanted to apply to the force.

Maybe the LAPD was a lame idea anyway. My parents just keep shaking their heads saying they can't figure out why I always have to make things so hard for myself. And of course Sarah loves how much trouble I'm in now. Like I'm proving even more how opposite we are—the shining star and the bad ass criminal.

April 21

Out of nowhere in my Life Skills class today something pops into my head. Even though you are on my mind all the time, I've never really thought about who the father was. I mean he obviously must have been a bastard or else why wouldn't he have stayed with you and married you and kept me? So how can I think of him as my father—or even have a picture of him in my mind? I can't believe he would be like any of the deadbeats at school who get their girlfriends pregnant and then dump them. And take pride in their stupid petty crimes. Maybe I'm not one to talk about low-lifes since I've got an official parole officer now. And my parents are avoiding me like I'm some kind of Alcatraz convict.

April 25

Gabriela, Gabriela. I love the sound of that name. I never thought I'd have anything to do with a girl at this school, because they're all just prostitutes in training. But then Gabriela shows up in my history class today—a transfer from somewhere near San Diego. I know you would love her too. She's beautiful. Like a Mexican angel. It's her first day and she already raises her hand to answer a question. Of course she's the smartest one in the class, way smarter than me. And shy too, which I love. I looked at her real intensely from across the room, and she didn't look back, but when the bell rang I went up to her and asked if she wanted me to show her where her next class was. When she said, *Sure, that'd be great,* her eyes froze onto mine. Now I have to wait two days to see her in history again. Gabriela, Gabriela…honey, you are worth the wait.

April 27

She has two little brothers she has to take care of in the afternoons, but I convinced her to go to In 'n Out with me after school today, promising I wouldn't make her late. She asked me where I was planning to go to college and what I was going to study. I told her I'm thinking about taking pre-engineering at Santa Monica College and then transferring to UCLA. That little twist of the truth put a beautiful smile on her beautiful face.

May 10

Respectful. That's the word she used. *You're respectful of me, which is why I like you so much, Jake.* She said that tonight on the phone. And I do respect her. Because I can tell she thinks highly of herself but in a good way, without being a snob. In fact she wants to help kids who live in bad neighborhoods once she gets her degree. She told me she even wants to open up her own school one day. She thinks so seriously about things. And then there are those muy bonita eyes of hers that look at me with a kind of sadness. It's like she understands the hard things people have to go through that they can't always talk about.

May 22

We talk on the phone every night and now I can look at her picture while we're talking. Today we went into one of those little photo booths at Santa Monica Pier. Put our faces close together. It almost looks like we're related, the olive skin, dark eyes and straight black hair. In the photos we're a real couple.

June 3

I don't go around telling people about my private life, but Gabriela and I basically almost had sex tonight. We were at her place babysitting her brothers and her mom wasn't coming home until after midnight. Up until tonight I knew she didn't want to go too far yet. But tonight she did want to. I love her, and I don't want to push her into anything she doesn't want to do, so we stopped before we got to the end. And I'm fine with that because she's a classy girl. But maybe even what we did was too much for her, because she seemed upset when I left her place. I hope she's okay, because tonight was like something holy to me—and I could never think of it any other way.

June 6

I think Gabriela feels bad about what we did last weekend, even though it was the most beautiful night of my life. She's avoiding me at school now. And tonight when I called, her mother told me she was busy. Benny thinks I should just leave her alone for a while, that girls don't like it when you pressure them too much. Like he knows all about it at fourteen.

June 13

One line stands out in Gabriela's letter. *You seem to need more from me than I can give you, Jake.* That sentence is too harsh for me to think about.

July 2

I saw Gabriela's mom today at Jamba Juice, where I've been working since school got out. She said hello but didn't mention anything about the break up. I still keep the two photos in my wallet—two of the four that we took at the pier. Gabriela was laughing and I'm standing behind her and her long hair is almost covering my face, like a little curtain I'm peering out of. Maybe she'll feel sad when she looks at her two photos that match up with mine. Those are the ones where her eyes are closed and I'm holding rabbit ears over her beautiful head just before I lean in to kiss her.

July 10

I knew Jamba Juice wouldn't prosecute—they just gave me a lot of shit over nothing. I was only ten dollars short, and for that they decide to fire me? I was going to pay it back the next day anyway, but they had me on camera putting the money in my pocket. Big deal. It was a rip-off place to begin with. Five bucks for a berry shake with a measly spoonful of yogurt. I'd rather go out with Rabbi Feinman than any of the rich, snotty girls who come into that pit. None of them could ever come close to Gabriela. My parents are hyper focused on the fighting in Israel and worrying about Sarah so they barely said anything about it. More head shaking, and that's about it. Anyway, my plan now is to take this paramedic course at Santa Monica College so I'll be part of the emergency medical team for the LAFD. It's kind of hard because I have to memorize all this physiology, but once I get the license I'll be pretty well set. Aside from being good at mechanical and technical stuff, I've always liked the idea of helping people in an emergency.

August 15

I dropped by Rabbi Feinman's cramped little office today. We were talking about nothing really, and then I told him about Gabriela and how she let me go after we had gotten so close. I told him I had been getting up my nerve to tell her the truth about my not really taking pre-engineering—because I thought she finally loved me enough to understand. And Feinman just listened to me, nodding his old bearded head. The only thing he said was *Sounds like you've suffered a big loss, Jake.* And then, for some reason, I don't know why, I showed him your photo, like I wanted him to see where I really come from. The only other person I'd ever shown it to was Benny, a long time ago when we were kids. So of course Feinman asks me about you, and I tell him all I know is your photo and that I don't even know if you live in L.A. anymore but I'm going to try to find you after my birthday, which is in only a month. So then he asks me what I hope will happen when I finally find you, and I say it will open a door that's been slammed shut. And then he doesn't really say anything, just looks at me with his dark watery eyes, like he's looking inside me. So now I have this big sad feeling about the whole thing where before it was something hopeful and private that I dreamed about whenever things got rough.

August 16

Here's what I think happened. I think my parents were never hot for each other, they just needed each other to have a kid. And they couldn't so then they got me and they were maybe kind of happy but then Sarah entered the picture and she's what they really wanted all along. So maybe there was no point in the whole adoption thing, even though they probably love me in their own weird way. I don't really feel sorry for myself because I've pretty much had it made, but

I think if you could have kept me, if you would have had a decent husband instead of whatever joker probably was my father, if you could have kept me I might have helped you with whatever problems you had and you would have been happy to have a kid, and we would have been there for each other.

August 23

Sarah sent me a photo of her and her girlfriends outside some café in Jerusalem, and another of an Israeli ambulance so I can compare it to the ones I'll be training with. Pretty thoughtful of her got to admit.

September 3

I saw my first dead body. There was an accident on Olympic just east of Robertson, a bad one, and the EM team had just arrived. The dead woman was a pedestrian run over by some kids in a Range Rover. Pretty badly mangled. It was weird because at first she almost looked like my mom. She was holding the same style handbag and the scene of the accident was only four blocks from our apartment. I don't know why but I took a photo of the body. Then I called my mom just to hear her voice.

September 21

Happy Birthday to me. Today's the day I've been counting down to for a year since my mom told me I could try to look you up when I turned eighteen. Maybe I'll call the adoption agency on Monday once I get up my nerve. Mom and Dad are taking me out to dinner tonight, but today I was on my own. I drove downtown to Olvera Street and bought myself a birthday burrito at one of those little outdoor stands. Looking around at all the Mexican faces I wondered if any of the women could be you. Like there aren't thousands of other places you could be in this city—if you're even here at all. There was a stand across from where I was eating where they sell colorful hats and piñatas, and I watched all these families with kids who would come by and point at their favorite piñata. And then I saw this beautiful young mom and her baby. The baby was crying and twisting around in his stroller like he wanted to get out, while the mom tried on all these straw hats and smiled at herself in the mirror, like she was flirting with herself. She was so pretty you couldn't blame her. Her red lips were the shape you make right before you kiss someone. She kept turning her head from side to side to see which angle was more flattering. The baby kept crying and the mom just kept looking into the mirror like he didn't exist. But she was so beautiful I had to take her picture.

Weight

Weight

When my mom met the guy my brother is currently seeing, the first words out of her mouth were: *Those cheekbones!* She can't help focusing on the aesthetics of someone's face or body: she's an artist. *I loved your father's burnt umber eyes and Michelangelo shoulders,* she has told me more times than I need to hear. So when I invited Marlon to come home with me this weekend, I knew Mom would be horrified. Maybe that's why I couldn't wait for them to meet.

Marlon doesn't carry himself like a fat person. He has perfect posture, a confident stride and a self-assured expression. But he doesn't take himself too seriously even though he has every right to since he's studying serious stuff. When I first met him I was impressed by his almost feminine listening skills. Not something most twenty-year-old guys come equipped with. Or fifty-year-old men, judging by my dad. When we got together for only the second time, he had remembered everything I'd told him the night we met about my band, wanting to check out the music scene in Iceland, and wishing I could wean myself from my obsessive need to run six miles a day. Our follow-up chat proved he had taken in every word: *So did you give in to the six-mile compulsion? Any new Reykjavikian bands on the horizon?* His sea green eyes and thick black eyelashes added to the intrigue, and I couldn't wait to run my fingers through his silky brown hair that shines like a shampoo ad. The supersized body didn't bother me at all; in fact, I found it aesthetically fascinating.

I'm not into appearances the way my mom is. She even makes spiritual decisions based on beauty – or the lack of it. Like the reason she doesn't go to the Catholic church that's closest to where my parents live. It's too homely for her. She actually refers to it as "the ugly church" because she thinks the Stations of the Cross look like pre-fab artwork from K-Mart. And the fixtures are too clunky. And the statue of Mary is in the parking lot overlooking a noisy bus stop. *It's hideously tacky, Dalia,* she shot back at me when I tried to shame her into feeling guilty for shunning the ugly church. She won't admit it, but another reason she won't go there is that the congregation is made up of plain, uninspiring people. Not poor or ethnic enough to be exotic and not hip or well off enough to be creatively dressed and groomed. In other words, not the cool people who attend the church she prefers. *I can't help it*, she says, *it's uplifting to see people in attractive clothes with healthy, beautiful bodies and faces.*

Throughout my adolescence my mother continually drove home a fact that I am completely unimpressed by: *You know you're exceptionally beautiful, don't you, Dalia?* she would ask rhetorically as she watched me getting ready to go out when I still lived at home. *You're prettier than me, a classic beauty. I'm just average attractive.* Why would she make such a ridiculous comment and frame it like some kind of competition? And what did being pretty have to do with anything? It didn't reflect my efforts or talents or my character. Marlon appreciates those things in me. Beauty is beside the point.

Driving down to my parents' house early yesterday morning we talked about a fantasy trip to Iceland. Marlon would use part of his grant money and I'd save my waitressing tips. We'd stay out all night clubbing, drink *brennevin* and eat herring. Then make love in the hot springs. We pulled off the road to clench the deal, the first time we'd ever done it in the car. I wouldn't say I was all the way in love with him but I was getting there. I wished we were spending the weekend alone instead of with my parents, but it was my mom's birthday and I'd promised I would come …if I could bring Marlon. My dad was throwing a big party for her forty-fifth, with Indian food catered by Electric Lotus and live music by a sitar-player friend of theirs. Since my brother couldn't take the time off to fly out, my being there was extra important. *Your mom will be crushed if you don't make it* Dad said.

After our off the road session, Marlon re-buttoned his turquoise and cherry red Hawaiian shirt, with just a bit of his beautiful big chest showing. I had my hand on his twice-the-size-of-a-normal thigh as we headed down 101.

Hope you're not put off by my parents. My dad can be super self-centered around strangers.

Don't worry I'll be my abnormal charming self.

He'll ask you sarcastic questions, like what are the hottest job opportunities for a PhD in philosophy.

I'll just tell him I plan to be a pot farmer as a back-up.

He'll definitely admire you for that.

I knew Marlon wasn't worried about meeting my parents. But he didn't realize that his weight would be a major issue for Mom. It would be all she'd be able to focus on when she met him—all 300 or so pounds of him. She wouldn't see his emerald eyes, black lashes or shimmering hair. She probably wouldn't even hear whatever engaging conversation he'd ease himself into because she'd be internally freaking out about her darling daughter dating a fat guy. Was I looking forward to it?

Mom registered no unusual reaction when she opened the door. And when we sat down at the coffee table over iced herbal tea, chips and salsa, there were no secret looks in my direction. No pursing of her pretty mouth into that pouty heart shape which she does when she's anxious. No indication that anything was in the least bit noteworthy about Marlon's size. Just the generic *Hey, Marlon, we've heard great things about you* from both her and Dad, and a rundown of the Indian menu. Then came the inevitable questions from Dad.

Actually, I'm doing my dissertation on a rethinking of the meaning of meaning—linguistics, semiotics, that sort of thing, Marlon told him, in answer to the *"which philosophers are you studying?"* question. *I'll refer to a number of different philosophers—the usual suspects…with a few twists. But tell me more about these focus groups you run.* My dad gets paid an inflated amount of money to organize focus groups for the movie industry so studios can figure out how to market their product.

It's fascinating, Marlon. What I do, in some small way I think, has a powerful influence on our core culture. Talk about meaning! I just did a picture with Steve Carell. Very deep film, which most people won't get, but it has the potential to be transformational if the right audience gets to see it.

I hate it when my dad uses that phrase *did a picture with* as if he directed the film and was close buddies with the star. He writes up a bunch of questions and decides which set of demographically correct people to ask them to. End of story.

While Marlon was getting the focus group tutorial, I saw him briefly glance over at one of my mom's famously weird paintings: a handsome-faced red devil, horns and all, with fiery arms outstretched towards an apparition of a honey-hued woman in swirling cloud-white gown. Mom noticed Marlon's attention to the painting and shot him a quick smile as my dad continued his movie marketing rap. She was turning in a remarkable performance of motherly calm, completely masking her shock at Marlon's heft. I could only guess at the comments she was drafting in her head for when we were alone. *So, what's the fascination, Dalia? Do you find that heft alluring—or is it p.c. to date a big guy?* The more I read her thoughts, the more I had to admit that I loved how distraught she was becoming thanks to my attraction to Marlon and my courage in bringing him to her undivided attention.

I love my mom, but her overabundance of talent, looks, and charisma which translate into her flawless ability to win people over has always seemed unfair. Although she's had to work hard to develop her artistic ability, it's her beauty that draws people in. I can see her charm in action even in her baby pictures that hang in my parents' hallway – the perfect oval-shaped face, the single dimple modestly set in her rosy cheek, the light shining through her intelligent dark eyes that seem to perceive life's most valued secrets. Her adorable face is nearly unchanged in the photo of her posing in front of a famous church in Rome where she traveled as a teenager. The only imperfection in her otherwise glorious smile is one eye-tooth crossing over her left front tooth just slightly—what my dad refers to as her *Natalie Wood tooth*. She has never had to use a lot of make-up, and even now wears only a simple lipstick and mascara, her smooth alabaster complexion untouched by the years. Her figure hasn't changed much either: largish breasts, small waist, and slim shapely legs that still look great in a bathing suit.

But my mom doesn't appreciate how lucky she is to have always been beautiful. And rather than show her gratefulness by ignoring other people's physical faults, she sees someone's bodily defects as a kind of karmic reflection of their character. It's as if she believes that bad skin or a crooked nose or a hump in one's back is punishment from God for a spiritual failing. *Oh my God,* she will say under her breath if we're out together and she spots some horrid defect, *look at the hideous scar on that woman's neck.* I remember feeling a pang of disappointment in her when I was a child and she pointed out that the President's wife was so much prettier than their unfortunate pre-teen daughter. I adored my beautiful, fun-loving, talented mom, but why did she have to mention the unattractiveness of a twelve-year-old with frizzy hair and braces? Where was her compassion? I have never understood why she can't get past a person's looks. But she seemed to be trying her hardest with Marlon, maybe because he was such a challenge. For someone like her, it must have been torture to try to ignore his immensity.

The party went smoothly at first. The obligatory birthday joints were passed around and my parents and their friends got embarrassingly high. Marlon and I had a few tokes just to be polite since getting stoned at my folks' party felt a little awkward. And I guess Marlon wanted to make sure he didn't get too loose with people he might want to favorably impress. We all sat at one long table and my parents came around with huge platters of the fifteen different entrees and side dishes they had ordered from Electric Lotus. I piled my plate with lamb bhuna, chicken vindaloo, vegetable masala, palak paneer, samosas, naan, raita, and more. Marlon focused on the tandoori tiger prawns. When my mom came by with the third round of main courses, she leaned in between me and Marlon and begged me to take the keema matar. *Sweetie, this is the best. You gotta have some. And you too, Marlon. My God, you've hardly eaten a thing. Here, I'm gonna give you some of this because I know you're both gonna love it.* And she proceeded to dollop huge portions onto our plates – two or three spoonfuls too many onto mine and way more than that onto Marlon's. He just sat there politely accepting what she was dishing out, while I tried to protest. *Mom, that's way too much. Stop.* But she wouldn't. And when there was so much food on Marlon's plate that it was oozing over the edges onto the Indian tablecloth, she looked at him and I knew exactly what was coming. I don't know how I intuited the precise words she would choose to humiliate him, but they flashed in my mind just before they popped out of her pretty mouth. *It's not like you can't handle it, right Marlon?* I could see his cheeks redden, but he smiled graciously, playing along as if he wasn't offended. *As a matter of fact, you're right, Eva,* taking a forkful of the spicy curried stew. *Wow,* he said, closing his eyes for effect, *now that's meaningful.* The whole table had quieted to hear his remark, an obvious reference to earlier table conversation centering on his dissertation topic, which my parents' friends had grilled him about. Now everyone was breaking up in exaggerated stoned laughter.

Meaningful curry – sounds like the title of a cookbook, one of my mom's friends offered. More stoned hilarity followed and then the birthday cake was brought out: multi-flavored frosted cupcakes arranged in larger-to-smaller circles and stacked on top of one another to form a towering cupcake tree. Two big number-candles in the shapes of a "4" and "5" perched on the uppermost little cake. My dad lit the "45."

Dalia, why don't you start us off, honey, my dad shouted. *She's starting a band…*

Actually dad, I'm thinking about it – haven't done it yet.

Well c'mon honey, your mom's waiting. I looked over at her, radiant in her youthful exquisiteness, her heart-shaped mouth air-kissing me as if her lips were made only for expressing motherly love.

Did she know how much I hated her for how she had just insulted Marlon, and for the unspoken judgments about him which I knew had been piling up in her head since we'd arrived? Still, I sang Happy Birthday in full voice as I watched Marlon savoring my every powerful note.

My dad fed my mom messy bites of cupcake as if it were their wedding day, then French-kissed the frosting off her lips. More joints were offered, more dopey laughter and sitar-playing until finally Marlon and I snuck out into the backyard without anyone noticing. It was dark and there was a cool breeze that felt great after the smoky closeness of the dining room. Two neighborhood dogs barked back and forth, one with a yapping little yelp, the other with a husky woof, neither managing to drown out my mom's party.

She's pretty vibrant for her age, Marlon said. I took off my sandals and felt the soft grass under my feet. We walked back to the far end of the yard and I plopped down under our giant Jacaranda, pulling Marlon down next to me. *Let's do it here*, I said. *I've never done it on home turf—or on a bed of purple petals.* His hair was blowing into his eyes and we pressed in close, each of us lying on our sides – face to face, belly to belly. *Well, my dear*, Marlon whispered, giving me little kisses on my forehead and eyelids, nose and cheeks, *allow me to initiate you.*

After the party guests had left and my parents had gone to bed, Marlon and I slipped back inside. My mom had made up the twin beds in my old room by pushing them together to make a queen-sized one. Pretty thoughtful of her. I was surprised that the weight thing hadn't been raised all afternoon when we were both getting dressed for the party. All she'd said as we bumped into each other in the hallway just before her guests arrived was *Lovely green eyes!* But she could only hide her disgust for so long until it had to spill out as she piled the curried stew onto Marlon's plate. Folded into his arms on my childhood bed, I knew I didn't belong in my parents' world. Their hip, artsy existence was wearing thin and not what I aspired to.

Marlon and I must have been entangled in similar erotic dreams. We grabbed each other in the middle of the night, the twin beds creaking in tandem. Lying there afterwards, I sang quietly into Marlon's ear, the beginning of a song I was working on. *Some guys are glued to the mirror. Some guys are glued to the screen. They're in love with their muscles or their money or their mother or their car or their dog or their gun. But you...inspire me, you...inspire me...*

Well, my little songstress, he whispered back, *you inspire me too.*

I was up early this morning but Marlon wasn't in bed. I put on my running shorts and shoes and made my way to the kitchen through the dark hallway. Maybe he was in the bathroom or waiting for me by the front door. We had talked about him using my old bike and joining me while I ran. *But don't count on it, my sweet,* he'd said, *six-thirty kind of cuts into my beauty sleep.* He wasn't in the bathroom and he wasn't by the front door.

Then I saw them standing by the breakfast room table, the first pale light breaking through the kitchen window. I couldn't tell who approached who first, but they moved toward each other as if it was the most natural thing in the world. And then they were embracing. Marlon held my mother like he was trying to console her. Her head was on his chest and he was stroking her hair. I heard a faint whimper but wasn't sure if it was her or me. And then they kissed, with no intention of malice.

Beef vs Tombaki Soul

Beef vs Tombaki Soul

We looked up to Beef but we also made fun of him. He was a pumped-up stuntman who spent his days working out in the driveway of our two-story apartment building. Lifting weights, jumping rope, push-ups, sit-ups, leg-lifts, rock-blue eyes focused straight ahead at absolutely nothing, especially not us pesky kids. Over-bulged muscles, stone-faced, unreachable. More mesmerizing than our video games.

Supposedly Beef got jobs on action movies but we'd never seen him in one and never managed to get an actual title out of him.

What movies have you been in, Beef?

You're too young to know 'em.

We're not that young!

I was eight and Tam was nine but that didn't mean we wouldn't have heard of anything Beef had been in. My dad and I watched a lot of action movies, old and new: the Rockys, Robo Cop, Die Hard, Terminator. And Tam came over a lot to watch with us. If Beef's movies had been popular, she and I would definitely have known the titles. So, he was either lying or the movies he was in never made it to the big time. Which gave us license to tease him, even though he could have pounded us with one finger.

Beef never seemed to have anywhere official to go during the day. Except on dates with hot babes. Actually, dates isn't really the word for it. Girls in shorts and high heels were always hopping down from his SUV in the middle of the day and following him up to his apartment on the second floor. The girls would wave at me and Tam with their silly little smiles like we didn't know what they were gonna do. Sometimes Tam and I hid in the bushes under Beef's window and heard the sounds coming from his bedroom. I wondered if I'd ever moan like Beef when I got older or have girlfriends like his.

I was the one who gave Beef his name. Even at eight I figured out that he was valued mainly as a hunk of muscular flesh, that he wasn't all that smart and had to rely on his strength and looks to get by. I thought it was funny, maybe even sad, that he didn't seem capable of carrying on an intelligent conversation with someone my age so I typecast him as an airhead. But I admired him for his discipline: seriously buff and committed to perfecting that body.

He acted as if he was trying to ignore us, but I think he basked in our attention. He'd bring his weights outside and pretend that his preferred work-out location was the driveway, that it had nothing to do with his adoring underage audience. Forever flexing and stretching and preening, he never said more than a few words. When we tried to engage him, he responded in monosyllables.

Been in any movies lately, Beef?

Nah.

Got any lined up?

Nope.

Dating any hot babes?

Uh huh.

What are their names?

None a your business.

We were awed when he proved his strength to us with so little effort, especially when he gave in to our pleading and lifted the two of us onto his monstrous shoulders. Tam and I thought he was a miracle man, even if he was more creature than human. We once saw him growl at a pit bull like they were family.

It was Tamara who got the idea of pitting Beef against Roshan, another neighborhood star—in our eyes anyway. Roshan and Beef were from different planets, but being around each of them was an otherworldly thrill, liberating us from our predictable parents. Tam's plan hit a nerve.

Let's see if Beef can actually fight—if he's really a tough guy or just faking it for the movies, she said. *I bet Tombaki Soul could take him no sweat.*

We called Roshan Tombaki Soul, or Soul for short, because he played a crazy Persian drum like it was his religion. He was a few years younger than Beef and much leaner, but he was in good shape. He ate healthy—mostly fruit and kabobs—and ran eight miles a day. He didn't have a job, just studied Torah and played his drum, which looked like a giant goblet. His parents didn't make him work because he was the youngest in the family, the last one living at home, and Torah study was enough according to him. *I was not made for the world of normal work* is what we overheard him telling a guy downstairs. Soul's arms and hands were so strong that he could go forever on his drum and never wear out. Sometimes he sat on the scruffy grass in front of our apartment building, tombak between his legs, and pound for hours. Eyes closed, he wouldn't even notice Tam and me fake belly-dancing in circles around him to his exotic beats. He was in his own personal drum-world.

Roshan's drummer muscularity was so impressive that a fight between him and stunt-guy Beef seemed pretty well matched.

He could turn Beef into hamburger, Tam claimed. Her Jewish bias was showing, but she also had a crush on Roshan. His olive-skin good looks and serene temperament were worthy of a Persian prince.

But do you really think Roshan would do it? I asked her.

Why wouldn't he? she snapped back.

The clash between the two brawniest guys on the block thrilled Tam, but I couldn't picture Tombaki Soul in a fight. His powerful arms were impressive pummeling his drum, but he was a peaceful guy. And Beef wasn't really a fighter either. As much as we pestered him about his movies and sexy girlfriends, it was hard to get him ruffled to the point of anger. We needed to figure out how to make the contenders mad at each other so they'd want to fight, but how? Brawling wasn't something you saw in our little slice of mid-city L.A. The neighborhood was mostly orthodox Jews, lower middle class Persians, starving actors, and young families in duplexes who couldn't afford a house yet. Yelling couples, crying babies, partying on weekends, but no physical fights in the eight or nine years of Tam's and my life on the block.

We couldn't come up with a way to entice Soul and Beef to fight each other, or to agree to a wrestling match that would prove their superior strength to us kids. But I hit on a less brutal idea. I'd seen the movie *Over the Top* with Sylvester Stallone, about this trucker who's a professional arm wrestler and tries to prove himself to his estranged son in an arm-wrestling match with a much heftier and meaner opponent. Sly almost gets demolished by the giant but of course beats him in the end. Even with his pit bull growl, Beef wasn't as nasty as the guy who nearly broke Sly's arm. But it would be exciting to watch him go arm to arm with Tombaki Soul. So how could we talk them into it?

We'd have to flatter Beef. Ask him in front of one of his girlfriends. Play like he was our hero and make it impossible for him to say no.

That wouldn't work with Soul, though, so Tam had an idea based on what her mom told her about the Persian synagogue Soul's family belonged to. They collected food and clothing for poor Persians in L.A. We could tell Soul that we'd go door to door and collect stuff for his temple if he won the arm wrestling contest.

Convincing Beef went as planned. As he and a new blonde girl—this one with a ponytail and purple leggings—left his apartment, we were waiting for them by his SUV.

Hey, Beef, our money's on you! I said, and laid out the plan for showcasing his amazing strength to his eager preteen fans. The girlfriend smiled, Beef smirked and shook his head.

Oh, yeah?

Tam and I smiled back at the girlfriend like two sweet little kids, and basically that was all it took. She gave Beef the *aww, aren't they cute?* look, and he had to demonstrate his soft side.

Hm, arm wrestling? Yeah, okay.

We told him to be out front on Sunday.

Persuading Soul wasn't as easy, but Tam targeted her pitch straight to her crush's generous heart.

It'd be a mitzvah if you won, Roshan, she said, casually throwing in the Hebrew word for good deed. *Think of all the people you'd be helping out.*

I don't wrestle. I'm a drummer, Soul said.

But it's only arm wrestling...and what about the poor Persians? They need clothes and food.

Soul considered the offer for a minute, his serious studious eyes drilling into ours.

You're right, he said, *it's an honor to help those in need.*

Of course, Soul had no idea that Tam routinely made fun of the homeless Persian lady who sold trinkets on the corner, calling her *loony lady* behind her back.

Sunday morning at ten. Card table and two chairs set up on the apartment front lawn. Kids from the block standing around waiting for the big event. No grown-ups except for the competitors and ponytail girlfriend.

Nodding politely at each other, no words uttered, Soul and Beef take their seats at the table. Beef's pale blue eyes stare blankly into Soul's intense brown ones. Tam starts them off:

May the best strong man win!

At first, they're evenly matched. Bent arms pivoting side to side on fixed elbows, neither forces the other to lose position. We hear their breathing between our cheers, most of us rooting for Roshan: *Way to go, Soul! Pound him like your drum! Where are your muscles, muscleman?*

A few minutes in, Beef pulls his move. Turning his palm toward his face and bending his wrist toward his shoulder, with seemingly little effort he muscles Soul's arm down flat. He repeats the move three times and it's over.

The two neighbor strangers stand up and nod at each other again.

Damn! Soul was just letting him win, Tam says so everyone hears. But I'd watched closely and knew it was Beef who held back. He was careful not to give it his all, didn't want to demolish Roshan— like the guy tried to do to Stallone—but just triumph enough to give us kids a kick.

Tam is bummed, but Soul takes the loss like a prince. *You're a strong guy,* he says to Beef, looking him straight in the eye. *Yeah, thanks,* Beef says, offering a polite nod. He and his girlfriend take off, and us kids beg Soul to go get his tombak and drum for us. *Not today, guys,* he says, *I have to study.*

About a year after the arm-wrestling affair, Tam's family bought a house and moved to the valley. I missed her. We were tight in a way that's nonexistent after puberty. Beef moved away too, but I never knew exactly when or where and never said goodbye. I eventually moved to the Bay Area for college and still live here. I think my parents mentioned that Roshan still lives in the neighborhood with his mom and dad.

So, it's about fifteen years since the strong guy match-up. I haven't heard from Tam in forever and she texts me a photo with a blurb about a guy named Nick Wild. Bare chested, bulging muscles, tattoos, bull dog snarl. It's Beef. He's dead. 38. Porn star. Opioid overdose.

Is everyone a porn star? Tam texts. *You can't just be a porn actor?*

They were both stars, I text back.

Who? she asks.

Beef and Tombaki Soul.

Bad Guitar

Bad Guitar

I t was a cruel set-up. God created Julian, beautiful Julian, only to doom him from the start. The first time I heard him I thought some twelve-year-old had just bought his first guitar and was lucky enough to hit a few near-chords by accident. Each strum whanged with angry energy but also a confident abandon, as if the guitarist had no idea how badly he was playing. There was a discernable rhythm, but it kept slipping off into its own lost territory.

Then there was the voice. Not so much singing as wailing. A pleading cry you would let loose only if you needed help. A sound that rockers try to achieve but usually have to fake. I couldn't tell if the bad guitar playing made the voice trail after it like a pitiful dog, or whether the dissonant voice made the guitarist sound even worse.

The two-story Spanish duplexes on our block are planted close enough to each other so that when one neighbor sneezes, yells at his girlfriend, or sings off-pitch, others can't help but hear. That is if the neighborhood kids aren't racing around on their scooters. Or the sirens aren't blaring. Or a police helicopter isn't homing in on a thief. The noisy mix was one of the reasons I rented here. I figured neighbors wouldn't be able to hear my practicing and wouldn't complain. As the violinist in an all-female mariachi band, I have to practice on my own at least an hour a day. And you can't play mariachi violin softly. That first day I heard Julian I was about to start practicing *La Malaguena*, but his voice upset me.

I couldn't concentrate so I made an espresso and took it out to my balcony where the voice came in more clearly. An odd melancholy version of an already melancholy Neil Young song. And there he was, sitting out on his second-floor balcony, thick chestnut hair falling onto his closed eyelids. Full lips opened painfully to expel the words. Lanky body hugging his beat-up Gibson. He was beautiful, way too beautiful for that voice. Hunched over in a cheap folding chair, his upper body bobbing back and forth, he sang the sixties song like he had been through it all back then. But he was barely older than me. Twenty-five at the most. And into sixties music like my mom. I tease her that she's stuck in a time warp. And she thinks it's quaint but sweet that I want to play in a mariachi band. Although she and my dad are both Mexican-American, I barely speak Spanish; but after studying classical violin, then ethnomusicology at UCLA, I heard recordings of Mariachi Vargas and was struck. This is me. This is what I was meant to do.

The way Julian gave in to that mournful song, it was clearly him.

A few days after I'd first heard him, I was rushing along the walkway on my way to a gig when he called out to me. My black charro suit stands out in this non-Hispanic neighborhood of mostly Middle Easterners, and the tight-fitting, silver-buttoned jacket and pants show off my curves. But that's not what Julian noticed.

You're a musician. I heard you practicing. He was standing on his balcony smoking, his voice sleepy and intimate; the hair still falling over his eye.

I looked up at him and introduced myself. *Hope I didn't bother you. I'm Linda. I moved in a week ago.*

In a good way.

What?

You bothered me in a good way.

He didn't smile, but I forced one, not sure of his meaning. *Thanks.*

Nice to meet you, Linda.

He slowly shook his brown head and opened his eyes wider, like a Disney prince snapping out of a bad spell.

Over the next few weeks I noticed that he lived with an older woman, and I couldn't help feeling dejected. Had I even admitted to myself that I was leaving a space for him, imagining something could happen between us? Then one night when the neighborhood noises died down, I heard their conversation and realized the woman was his mother. After that, whenever I heard them I could tell she was constantly badgering him—yelling at him to get ready for his appointment, for his class, to get in the car so they could go grocery shopping. He never seemed to go out with anyone else. No friends came by to see him.

About three o'clock one morning, I woke up and heard him singing. No guitar, just the voice. A meandering song, unrecognizable and unending. He was singing pretty loud but none of our neighbors were protesting. His wayward voice and endless stringing together of words made it hard to discern any distinct phrases, but I thought I heard the words "arriving" or "riding" or "sliding."

Marcela and I were practicing a few nights later when Julian knocked. I opened my door to find his sad, curious, too-handsome face, his lush hair unevenly combed back.

Can I come in and listen? He was wearing an old Blondie t-shirt and tight black jeans. He had a nice body, maybe a little too thin.

Marcela glanced at him, then me. Her look asked, who is this heart-throb and why haven't you told me about him?

Uh, sure. You a mariachi fan?

I don't know. What is it?

I told him Marcela and I would introduce him to our music, and he sat there on my couch more than an hour with his eyes closed, slowly nodding as we played *El Nino Perdido*. I liked having him there. Marcela and I would stop occasionally to talk about the piece or our performance, but Julian made no comments. Just sat there and listened. Sometimes he'd look at me, serious and questioning, but mostly his eyes were closed, lost in music he'd never heard before. Then someone knocked.

It was his mother, offering a flustered apology. *Sorry to interrupt.* She had come to claim her son, as if picking him up from a play date. *Hey, it's time to come home now*, she said to Julian, adding with a quick nod in my direction, *Thanks for having him over.* Julian glared at his mother and slowly got up from my couch. Then he looked at me for a few seconds without uttering a word. *Beautiful music*, he finally said. *Beautiful music.*

Marcela couldn't believe that a guy who looked like a roughed up, un-self-conscious jeans model was still living with his mother. *Well, a lot of young people live with their parents these days*, I defended. *...to save money.* I was trying to blot out Julian's mother from the romantic yet limited picture I had of Julian—a loner lost in his music...and now mine.

I heard him in the middle of the night again, his guitar resonating in short brash A-minor strums. I heard the words *granite*, as in the rock, and *granted*, as in don't take me for granted. Some angry comparison between the two. My take was that it was like a psychic protest song. He was mad at being taken for granted? His heart was made of granite? I wanted to close my window and go back to bed, but instead called out softly so I wouldn't wake anyone else.

Julian, what's going on? It's late.

He didn't hear me at first, still lost in the song.

Julian, it's me, Linda.

He finally stopped playing and looked toward my open window.

Linda, hi. Hello…I'll come over.

This was probably not good. The broken off bits of his song had wound their way into my brain, and I found myself improvising off his lead phrase. His rough voice and angry strums were inside my head. What was I doing? When he got to my door I told him to come in and I'd make some tea. While I boiled water, he sat on the couch admiring the artwork on my walls. A Gronk poster of a scarlet-faced man on a purple horse, a friend's watercolor riff on Frida Kahlo, and a poster from the Fowler Museum on carnival art. He liked the Gronk.

Where did you get this, Linda?

I picked it up downtown at one of those open studio events.

He looked at the poster and then at me, and then he gave a little laugh.

I like it. The colors are so bright.

The simplicity of his words didn't match what I saw as his intense focus and intelligent curiosity. He had looked at the poster like he truly cared about what it was trying to convey, and that was how he looked at me. Maybe it wasn't such a good idea to have invited him in. I was tired. And he was definitely strange in a way that wasn't familiar to me. But I wanted him there. I liked looking at him and having him look at me with those black, admiring eyes that seemed to search for what I was all about, beyond the charro outfit and the too-bright Latino art. He had me on a pedestal, but he was making me feel I had earned it. And he seemed perfectly content just to sit there in my presence drinking tea. No chit-chat. No expectations.

Well, I'd better go, he finally said after minutes of silent tea drinking. *Let you sleep. Sorry I woke you before, Linda.*

When he got up to leave, he gave me a barely noticeable smile that was unlike any I'd ever received from a man at that hour of the night. Wordless and intimate but polite, like a deeply felt thank you.

You busy on Sunday? I heard myself ask. *I'm playing at a family party. You could come.*

I could come with you?

Sure. Three o'clock.

I heard him the next night and the following two nights after that, sometimes moaning to his ragged guitar in long monotonic streams, other times just his pleading voice. Like sounds you make when you're tossing at night in the grip of a fever or lovemaking. I wanted to take back my invitation to the party. But how could I tell him that I'd made a mistake, that he was too weird even for me? I hadn't asked him, but as far as I could tell he didn't have a job. He mentioned that he was taking a class at City College, but he obviously wasn't a fulltime student. All of that, and even living with his mother, would have been alright if he'd been like other people I know who are trying to make it as musicians. But Julian was just this strange guy who sang to himself and played bad guitar on his apartment balcony. Handsome, polite, admiring of my music—but definitely not in my world. Which attracted and scared me.

The party was a *quinceanera* for my cousin, Natalie. The whole extended family would be there, along with a bunch of Natalie's fifteen-year-old friends. Natalie's dad, my Uncle Alex, had asked if I would play with my band to give the party an authentic flavor. *Otherwise we might as well wait a year and just throw her a sweet sixteen,* he told me, adding that Natalie had protested the traditional frilly dress and tiara, which she referred to as "too Mexican." I'm now the designated ethnic roots-provider in the family, which doesn't bother me. I love the music—and I would even if I were Swedish.

Julian wore a black fifties-style short sleeve shirt with a white stripe slashed diagonally across the chest. And the same tight black jeans. His hair was slicked back and gave off a flowery scent. On the way to the party, I explained to him that for Mexican girls their fifteenth birthday is a celebration of the journey from childhood to womanhood. He didn't seem interested and instead asked *how did you learn to play, Linda?* I told him I had studied classical violin when I was younger but fell in love with Mariachi music when I got to college. He told me he was taking a math class at Santa Monica College. I asked him what kind of math. *There are some mathematical theories that I'm working on,* he said. Being un-mathematical I couldn't ask him to tell me more because I wouldn't understand. So I asked whether he was planning to work at something related to his math studies. *I'm not sure if my theories are accurate but I have to keep working on more problems,* he said.

After I'd introduced him to my parents and aunts and uncles and cousins, including the birthday girl, I told Julian to make himself at home, get a plate of food and I'd come find him when the band took a break.

Our bass player asked *Who's the cutie?* as we were setting up. I looked over at him and wondered that myself. I've always believed that chemistry is more than just physical. You sense something in a person that pulls you in, something unfinished in yourself or …I hadn't figured it out but I wanted to because there had been some poor choices in my past. And I was being pulled in again now.

Tables were set up on the patio, guests were getting plates of food from the buffet, and Natalie's crowd of friends was congregating under the trees away from the grown-ups. We played *Jesusita en Chihuahua,* but I could tell my focus was drifting. Mariachi violin is like no other instrument. There's a unique excitement as the song builds toward an emotional high. I'm usually lost inside the music, the boundary between myself and my instrument falling away. But I wasn't there. I was drawn to Julian, wanting to watch him watching me. I was performing passably on my solo, but I wanted to find Julian's face more than I wanted to nail the piece. When the guitarist took her lead, I turned to the lawn chair where I'd left him but he wasn't there. Nor could I see his head among the sea of relatives at the buffet. During my lead again, I came in a fraction of a second late. I wasn't in my zone. I closed my eyes for a second to try to re-connect with *Jesusita,* which I managed to do for the last section of the piece. Then the applause and the whooping from Natalie's friends. *You ladies are hot!* a fifteen-year-old boy blurted out.

Relatives and friends of Uncle Alex and Tia Ana came up to kiss me and compliment the band. My dad gave me a crunching hug. *Linda, Linda, who would have thought you would be a mariachi – after all that Mozart stuff.* I still loved Mozart. I had since I was a kid younger than Natalie.

The sun was beginning to shift and I looked out past the patio where I could hear the clanging of the wind chimes Uncle Alex had hung from one of his orange trees. The kids were a blur of moving shapes, darkened by shadows cast by the citrus branches. I heard Natalie's laugh and the bluffing voice of a boy her age. A part of me felt I belonged more with the kids under the trees than the grown-ups at the party. It had only been a flash of time since I was fifteen.

Where's your friend? Marcela was taking bites from her plate of food.

I don't know. I haven't seen him since we started to play.

You serious about this guy?

Not really. I just thought he'd enjoy the band.

Right.

My Julian fascination was probably ridiculous. Who was he anyway? A beautiful boy-man who couldn't even play guitar. Sensitive but inarticulate and unschooled. He seemed to be attracted by my music, but what did I want from him? To sleep with him… and then what?

I glimpsed what looked like his silhouette at the far end of the yard near the swing set, beyond the tables that had been set up under the trees. The sun had gone down and it was almost dark up there now. If it was him, he and Natalie were standing near the swing set, their heads turned toward each other. It was windy and Natalie's long hair was blowing into her face.

It was Julian. I could tell as he turned slightly to reveal the outline of his long slim legs. Natalie swept the hair out of her face but the wind kept blowing it back. She lifted her hair into a temporary ponytail, leaving her arms raised gracefully above her shoulders. Marcela was talking to me but I hadn't heard what she'd said. Walking away, she repeated *We're on in five minutes.* I looked back up the hill. Julian had taken Natalie's hand and was helping her into a swing. He pushed her and she pumped her legs, riding the air back and forth.

I wanted to be Natalie. Julian was probably looking at her the way he'd looked at me the night we drank tea in silence, giving me his rapt, knowing attention. That's all I really wanted from him. Natalie probably didn't appreciate it at fifteen. Didn't know what it meant for a man to see you the way you want to be seen. But Julian was pushing Natalie in the swing, not me.

I had to do another set before the birthday cake was brought out. When we finished, I hardly heard the applause. I was scanning the area under the trees, now barely visible. The swing set was lost in the dark. A string of colored lights lit up the party patio as my aunt carried out the three-tiered pink and white birthday cake. She and my uncle called out, *Where's Natalie? Where's our birthday girl?* Heads twisted, guests trying to find my cousin. I wouldn't be the one to tell. A few of Natalie's friends whispered to themselves but didn't say anything. Then a boy yelled out, *She's up by the swings with some older guy!*

My uncle set down his camera and walked hurriedly up the hill. His shouts followed, then Natalie's. She dashed into the house and slammed her bedroom door. In all the commotion, and with the aunts trying to serve coffee and cake despite Natalie's absence, I never saw Julian leave. I looked for him, but he was gone.

It's been a month since the party and Julian is still missing. Although I can't stop blaming myself, his mother doesn't hold it against me. *It's happened before*, she said. *He'll get upset about something and run off—for weeks, maybe months.* I asked her why. *I overdid it a little with the drugs when I was pregnant with him and that led to some of his mental problems. Without his meds he loses it and who knows where he'll end up.* She told me the last time Julian ran off he got arrested for breaking through someone's window and taking a bath. When the people came home and found him in the tub, they were terrified—even though Julian didn't mean any harm.

I try to picture Julian as a complete stranger and how I would react finding him in my bathtub, a broken window shattered on the floor. What would I do if I found him playing his bad guitar and singing in a voice only God or a lover could adore?

Two Freakin' Words

Two Freakin' Words

He dishonored us and it was all because of that girl. Maybe it's like the Bible said, you shall leave the home of your parents and make a new home with your wife or something like that. But he totally disowned us and I prayed about it ever since he met her, that he would not marry her, that he would see that she isn't right for him, but he got his heart broken two times before because they were beautiful girls and that's why he chose this girl because she's not attractive and he told me he would feel safe with her, she would never leave him, but now look what happened! Our family is torn apart and I know my husband isn't perfect but that wasn't my fault and I didn't say anything to hurt anyone's feelings, in fact I took her out to dinner to the Cheesecake Factory, the whole family came so we could meet her and my husband wasn't working at the time so I paid and I work really hard for my money but did she say a word at the dinner, no, she just sat there and ate her food and acted like we weren't even there, and I know my son wanted someone like her, someone quiet because he's quiet too and he was a virgin when he married her, twenty-eight, never drank, never took drugs, never swore, and even I did things when I was young that I'm not proud of, and I know my husband's not perfect I've told him that he shouldn't talk that way to me either because that's not what the Bible tells you to do. You're supposed to honor your wife, I don't remember the exact words but it's in there. But my son hates him so much that he changed his name so that it's not his father's name anymore, and it's all because of her and her feelings but what about our feelings and our family, a family that believe me I almost broke away from myself after my husband cheated but I told him I wouldn't let that tear our family apart because my father left my mother for another woman and after that my mother had to work two jobs and never got a penny from my father who married somebody else and had children with her and never kept in touch with us so I told my husband I'm not going to let you leave me, I'm not going to divorce you for this because it's not what's in the Bible, I don't think, even though I'm not a Catholic but I don't believe in divorce anyway. But if my son stays married to this girl it will be a tragedy because it's already a tragedy and I told him she was not right for him and I've prayed about it and God tells me to just have faith and I'm trying, so when I wrote to my son and asked him to come for Christmas with his wife and I never heard back from him, a few months later I wrote to him again and asked him to come for dinner and never heard back from him and I was just about finished with the whole freakin' thing because I'm reading this Christian self-help book that tells me to love God and also to love myself and tells me what to do for my self-esteem because this thing with the girl and my son was a slap in the face to my self-esteem so I'm praying and putting it in God's hands but it's really hard to stop thinking about it so I started calling my son at work begging him to come to brunch on Mother's Day when we always go to the Cheesecake Factory, the whole family, and he says something like how insulting it was that his father said that, and I tell him that his father didn't actually say it to the girl just to him, just those two little words and if they got repeated to her then maybe she's just too sensitive and being too sensitive is not good for your self-esteem, believe me I know. I told him you're still my son and there was silence on the other end of the phone and I told him remember when we used to go to church together just you and me when no one else in the family would go and now I go by myself and pray that you will be part of the family again but instead you are part of her family, that girl that you don't have anything in common with even if she's a Christian too but her weight, oh God her weight and there is still silence on the other end of the phone. And I say was it really so terrible what your father said that you had to change your name and not come to church with me or go to the Cheesecake Factory anymore, and then he just said the two freakin' words that changed everything: fat pig. And then he hung up on me even though I wasn't the one who said that about the girl it was my husband and he didn't say it to her face only to my son who shouldn't have mentioned it to her anyway and I have put up with a lot worse from his father than two little words but I put up with it and try to keep up with my self-esteem even though my son will never change his mind about the girl who is way too overweight for him and never joined in the conversation or tried to act friendly to our family when I took her out to dinner at the Cheesecake Factory which was before she even heard the two freakin' words.

Diosa

Díosa

It was my smile on the day she joined the club that made her choose me to do special favors for her. It was because I was so happy that Ray would be picking me up after work and taking me to a movie, so I was smiling to myself even before Sandra approached me. That smile—which was for Ray not her—was my biggest mistake, even though smiling politely is part of my job. It lets the ladies know we are glad to make the locker room sparkle for them. Some guests smile back when they see me but most don't see me. They glance only in the glamourous mirrors as they rush to work out or head for a shower.

Smile politely, be friendly, but do not bother the guests. Do not talk to the guests unless they ask you for something and then let them know you will be glad to do whatever they ask. And do it quickly because they are busy people. Your job is to make sure they thoroughly enjoy our premier class fitness club. Premier class service and amenities are what make our club special.

That's what is written in the employee guidelines.

My job is eight hours cleaning the toilets, sinks, mirrors, floors, and the beautiful private shower stalls lined with green jewels. That's what the small rectangular tiles in the shower seem like to me. I like to run my hand along the glassy shine after I scrub them and imagine that those elegant jewels are in my bathroom at home. The gym ladies do not like to go into a shower stall that is wet from someone else's shower, so I am quick to wipe down the floor and walls after anyone uses it. I wrap a thick towel at the bottom of my mop and carefully sop up any leftover water. Sometimes there are hairs, disposable razors, bobby pins, or clumps of shaving cream or hair conditioner on the tiled floor of the shower, so I wipe it down and pick up everything to make sure that the stall is dry and beautiful again. I also fill up the stainless-steel bottles of expensive shampoos and conditioners and liquid soap that hang in every stall. I love breathing in the fruity smell of the steamy air after a client has showered. The liquid soap smells like grapefruit only sweeter, like the little white flowers on the grapefruit tree in my abuela's backyard in Indio.

Most of the ladies' bodies are firm and slim like my oldest daughter who is fourteen. It's funny to me that they use the words work out. Sure, they sweat when they exercise on those machines but I doubt they would want to do the work that makes me sweat: the showers, the toilets, the sinks, the floors. I'm sure they hire someone to do that work for them in their own homes. My work, what I do—it's not exactly exercise but I can feel my muscles working when I push the mop and scrub the tiles and toilets. It doesn't make me slim, but I don't mind. I'm curvy and Ray likes me this way. *You are my goddess, mi diosa,* he tells me. Even though he exaggerates, I love his romantic words.

Six months ago when Sandra joined the club, she asked *Would you do a few special favors for me?* and I have been doing them every day since: Leave a stack of fresh towels in front of her locker before she arrives so she doesn't have to think about grabbing them herself. Get her a terry robe from the guest laundry room, so she won't have to go get it herself like the other members. Fold the robe neatly and leave it on top of her stack of towels. (Most members take one or two towels but Sandra likes four.) Wipe down her locker so it is perfectly sanitary and clean.

Sandra calls me Tiffy. My mother gave me the name Tiffany because she thought it sounded typical American and I'm fine with it but I don't like Tiffy. Sandra talks to me in a high little voice, as if I were her child. *Hi Tiffy! Good morning, Tiffy.* I give her a soft smile, friendly but not too friendly.

When I tell my sister about Sandra calling me Tiffy and all the extras I do for her, she gets angry with me and we go through it.

She treats you like a slave

Not a big deal.

But you're not her personal servant, Tiffany.

So what am I supposed to do, tell her I can't get the towels for her anymore or wipe down her locker or fold her robe?

She'll live.

Yeah, but she wouldn't be happy.

So why do you care, Tiff?

Why do I care...

It can be embarrassing when another maintenance worker hears Sandra talking to me with that sugary voice: *Thank you, Tiffy! You are the best!* I just smile and set down the stack of towels and try to avoid my co-worker's disapproving stare.

Last month, two days before Christmas, Sandra had an extra-big smile on her face when I passed by her locker pushing my mop. *Oh, there you are! Come here, Tiffy, I have something for you!* She handed me a gift bag with red and green tissue paper puffing out of it and her eyes got wide as I took it from her and smiled my smile. *I want you to open it now, Tiffy!* Sometimes clients give us a box of

See's candy at Christmas or a twenty-dollar gift card. I use the cards to buy my kids things. As I pulled the tissue paper from the bag, Sandra looked like an excited parent waiting for her kids to open the biggest present under the tree. *I got it at Bloomingdale's, Tiffy. Do you like it?* The sky blue cashmere sweater was beautiful. *I love it. Thank you, Sandra.* She put her arms around me and squeezed so tight it made me cough. Then I smiled big for her. I wore the sweater on New Year's Eve and Ray told me I looked like a dream.

Yesterday I heard Sandra talking in front of the make-up mirrors about an argument she had with the valet at a restaurant on Beverly Drive. *He told me they only take cash and refused to let me use my American Express,* she said. *These little valet guys telling me what to do? Who do they think they are?* The ladies standing beside her at the mirrors didn't say anything. Just raised their eyebrows and finished blow-drying their hair. But Sandra didn't mind that nobody was agreeing with her. Of course, I could not tell her that my father is a valet in West Hollywood. I don't know if the company he works for allows customers to use their credit cards. All I know is that sometimes his tips are pretty good. Ray was thinking of working there too but he makes better money painting houses and getting paid under the table. Sometimes he makes over a hundred and fifty dollars a day. *Those damn little valet guys, I swear,* Sandra said. *I'm not going back there ever again!*

Why did she call them little valet guys, my sister asked when I told her about Sandra's temper tantrum. *I don't know, maybe they were short,* I said. *I doubt that's what she meant,* my sister said, giving me a disgusted look. *How can you put up with her? Why don't you just tell her to get her own lousy towels?* My sister isn't the only one who gets upset about Sandra. One of the guys who works at the front desk told me she had a fit when a make-up mirror lightbulb went out last week. *She's a class-A bitch*, he said. But when she screamed at him he just smiled and got someone to change the lightbulb.

I don't know why Sandra got so mad about the lightbulb or the valet guy. Or why she loses her temper at the women in the laundry room when there's a tiny stain on her towel. Or at the other maintenance girl who fills in for me on my day off and forgets to leave Sandra her stack of towels like I do. I used to think she had a hard job and that's why she loses her patience a lot, but I heard two gym members saying that Sandra doesn't work, that her husband supports her. *So what does she do other than work out*, one said. *Probably finds valets to terrorize*, the other one whispered.

Sandra exercises every morning for an hour and a half and has the muscles to show for it. Every day she wears a different pair of brand new Nike shoes in every color of the rainbow. She can do whatever she wants after she leaves the club because she doesn't have to work. And I heard her say she never wanted kids. So she's totally free. I don't think any of the ladies she talks to in the locker room are her friends. And I doubt if her husband treats her as nice as Ray treats me because I know she's not happy. If she was, she wouldn't get so angry all the time over the stupidest little things.

She doesn't get angry at me. I make sure of that. She smiles when she finds the neatly folded stack of towels I leave for her every day. And when I watch her check to make sure that the terry robe I left for her is absolutely clean, with no spots, and that I have wiped down her locker so that it's germ-free, she smiles again.

This morning, as soon as she sees me, she waves and calls out in her baby voice: *Hi, Tiffy! How you doin?* I am the only one she talks to this way, the only one she softens for, the only one with the power to sweeten her.

Ray says I'm an angel. My sister calls me a slave.

Good morning, Sandra, I say. And I smile at her without really faking it.

The First

The First

We were only unequal in ways that didn't matter. I had a mother and you had a Jesus on the top bunk. When you were at my house, my mom treated you like another daughter. She considered your dad a close friend and admired him for doing what no other dads did in those days— shopping and cooking, washing and ironing your clothes, signing your report cards, and always being an enthusiastic audience during the plays we put on in your backyard for him and my mom: *Clues in the Barbeque Ashes, Mystery of the Golden Roller Skate,* and *Girls Who Sing Upside Down.* You not having your own mother? You never brought it up.

We didn't have to decide who was who. We were both. We switched back and forth without really thinking about it. One day you were Nancy Drew and I was George, her best friend. The next day I'd be Nancy and you'd be George—or Georgia, the weird name she was born with. We weren't mimicking anything from the book, we were acting out our own mystery. That was the thrill. Making up our own story as it unraveled, effortlessly falling into it and into our characters. Part them, part us.

It was always your backyard, not mine. Mine was bigger but flatter and too many flower beds. Yours was more fun. Craggy avocado tree, overgrown hill that sloped down from your small mint green house, rusty garden tools, clothes line with a drooping bag of clothes pins, and Trev, your aging black cocker spaniel who trailed behind us wherever the clues led. If you were the first to identify a clue, you'd announce in an eerie voice: *Nan-cy, cloo-ooze, white dog doo!* And I'd race over from the other end of the yard where I was also searching for suspicious objects. I'd slowly walk around the fossilized dog droppings, inspect them, kick them, and seriously consider what they could mean. *They've been here a long time, George, so the creature must be dead by now,* I'd say. *We'd better check behind those bushes.* We'd run over to the bushes that your father had warned us about, (*Don't eat the berries, they're poisonous.*) and if we didn't find anything there, we'd follow another mysterious sign. *These must be the footprints of the woman with no voice, who stares but never speaks,* you'd say. And I'd keep it going: *You're right! She was up to no good. And her high heels fit these prints. We must find her!*

Without a pause, you would take it from there. You'd point to the old lady hanging up her laundry next door and come up with reasons why she was most likely the villain. You'd whisper: *I've seen her bony, yellow fingers with pointy nails, and she gives me the evil eye when I'm riding my bike.* Then I'd turn to notice another obvious clue: a torn nightgown hanging from your clothesline. *That's hers! How did it get there, George? We have to investigate!*

When the sun was on its way down and your father called us in for dinner, we hadn't exhausted the mysteries. There were always more strange objects, unexplained coincidences, shady suspects.

I loved your dad's dinners. I liked that he brought us our plates already filled—with meat, potatoes, vegetable—rather than platters in the middle of the table like at my house. There were more people in my family than in yours, but I liked that at your house we were the unrivaled focus of your dad's attention. Just me and you. I loved his pork chops with gravy and buttery mashed potatoes. You made jokes about the apron he wore over his shirt and tie and about him being a good cook. He was an embarrassment for you because he was old enough to be your grandfather and because men weren't supposed to do the cooking. My father only cooked one thing: scrambled eggs on Sundays. But your dad did all the cooking all the time because he was the only parent in your house.

I did ask you once about why you didn't have a mother. You had one, you told me, *but I never see her and it's okay*, you said. *Doesn't she want to see you?* I asked. You told me she had come around a few times to spy on you at our school playground. But you ignored her and never went over to the fence where she called to you. *She's just a crazy lady*, you said, like it was no big deal. I didn't ask you anything else. I could tell you were done talking about her. We were seven then, and you never mentioned her again.

Then there were the things you had that I didn't. But because I was at your house as often as at my own, I thought of those things as mine too. Like your redwood bunk beds. Taking turns sleeping on the top happened without us having to negotiate. As many nights as I slept up there, the top bunk was always a thrill. Climbing the ladder, hitting my head on the ceiling, being above it all. And the small framed picture of Jesus—blonde and serious—on the wall of the top bunk. He was another bunkmate. The bottom bunk was like sleeping in a cave. Dark and close. When I slept on the bottom, I loved to hear you singing to yourself at night or rolling over just above me, making the bed boards creak.

We never referred to the Jesus. Neither you or your father seemed religious, so I wasn't sure why he was up there anyway. Sometimes when you got mad—you'd accidentally drop a box of Cheerios and the O's flew across the floor, or Trev slobbered all over your new pedal pushers—you'd shout "Jesus H. Christ!", pause to look over at your dad, and then you'd both burst out laughing. Still, the top bunk Jesus left an impression. No matter how many nights we stayed up laughing so loud that your dad had to knock on the wall to quiet us down, and as many times as we got away with stealing candy bars from the hall cupboard and bringing the stolen goods back to our bunks, blonde Jesus remained solemn and calm.

We were still bunkmates in seventh grade when you started going for drives with Barry after school. This was long after our practice sessions touching tongues so we'd both be ready for boys. And it was a few years after we'd gotten our hearts broken when we saw Fabian in the flesh in a restaurant where my older sister was having her sweet sixteen party. He refused to give us an autograph and was crushingly unattractive anyway, nothing like his photos, which made us doubt the authentic lovability of celebrities. *Jesus H. Christ, what a loser,* you said. *How could anybody kiss him with all those pimples,* I said.

Barry was older than us, one of the cool guys from the high school we were still a few years from attending. We saw him at a coffee shop near our junior high, and all it took was just one look, as the song predicted. After grabbing the seat next to you at the counter, he asked if chocolate was your favorite flavor. When you nodded and gave him the look, he won you over with his ESP: *I could tell*, he said. He ordered chocolate shakes for both of us, paid the check, and that was it.

Your dad didn't know that several times a week Barry gave you rides after school and that you were making out with him at the beach. I was excited for you and glad to be the excuse for why you got home late. You explained to me how making out with Barry was different than when we touched tongues as young girls. *His tongue goes all the way inside your mouth,* you said, which sounded weird, *and then you do it back to him.* I asked you if it felt gross and you said he did it gently so you liked it. We weighed too much now for us both to sleep on the top bunk like we did sometimes when we were younger. But once in a while we'd sleep on the bottom together and we'd touch each other's developing breasts. *Does Barry do it like that,* I'd ask. *Much better than that,* you said, and we laughed too long and too loud until your dad started knocking on the wall.

Unlike my dad, who went to work in an office every day, your dad stayed at home. He was retired, you said, and got a check every month for the years he spent in the costume departments at movie studios. He'd tell us stories about all the old movie stars, most of whom we'd never heard of except for Doris Day and Marilyn Monroe. One actress had such big breasts, he said, that her bras had to be designed by her boyfriend who built airplanes. We didn't really believe that, but it was a funny story. And since we were in the throes of buying our first bras, we could relate. *Think Barry could design a good bra for you?* I asked. *Maybe he could make two—one for each of us. Actually,* you said, *he probably could—he draws cartoons, sexy ones, too.*

Barry was not only a good cartoonist; he was handsome and confident. We both admired his smooth skin and silky hair and slim body. He told you he was going to be in politics one day, which was why he was running for class president and had to give a speech in front of the whole high school. He practiced on you as he drove you home the day before the assembly. *Who knows,* you told me on the phone that night, *maybe I'll run for mayor of L.A. one day. I know I could make a good speech.* I knew, even then, that you were daring enough to do whatever sparked your imagination.

At thirteen, I wasn't exactly trailing behind you when it came to my attraction to boys, but my intensely felt crushes never amounted to anything tangible. As for making out, I had never made it past public kisses at spin the bottle parties. I had yet to be invited to take a ride to the beach alone with a high school boy. I don't think it was because you looked older. It was that you knew how to act older, which was why Barry wanted you and not me. Would I have gone with him if he had asked? Hearing your beach stories whispered to me on the bottom bunk, feeling both envious and relieved that it wasn't me French kissing an older boy, I still don't know how terrified or ecstatic I would have felt alone in the car with Barry. But it almost *was* me since it was happening to you.

Overhearing your end of one of our phone calls about Barry, your dad confronted you. He was more tolerant than my dad would have been, but he was upset that you had lied about where you were after school. He didn't forbid you from seeing Barry, but he wanted to meet him.

That's not gonna happen, you told me at one of our last sleepovers. *My dad is living in the dark ages.* I didn't understand why you didn't want your father to meet Barry, but of course I was on your side. *We'll figure it out,* I said. You looked at me with that look you would give your dad whenever you planned to defy him. *We?* you said.

Barry continued to come by our junior high after school. The two of you would talk for a few minutes, and then he'd drive away. Were you planning something? Meeting secretly somewhere? You never told me, and without discussing it we began a heartbreaking new routine: I no longer came to your house after school and you didn't come home with me. The sleepovers didn't happen anymore, and the phone calls tapered off. I missed you terribly but imagined you off in some hidden place with Barry and was rooting for you. One day at lunch I asked if you'd figured out a way to see him. *Don't worry, I won't ask you to lie for me anymore,* you said. You didn't sound like yourself. *I'm not worried,* I said. I was talking to someone who looked like you, but you were gone.

We moved on, as people now say. You had many boyfriends; I had a few. You sang your own songs at our high school talent show. I worked on the school paper. I went to college. You travelled to India and Nepal. We kept in touch every so often but rarely saw each other.

Because of what your son has asked of me, I've been thrown back to our girlhood searching for clues to unresolved questions: who made the first move when we were seven? what drew us to each other? why was our friendship as exhilarating as a romance, but so much easier? what was it about us together that made me crave spending every free moment with you?

I always assumed that what made us inseparable was how alike we were. But that's not really the way it was. You shouted *Jesus H. Christ!* I felt reverent on the top bunk, even though I'm Jewish. You laughed when you rammed into a garbage can on roller skates and broke your arm. I was secretly scared of the trampoline but faked it every day in the summer before fifth grade so you could do your wild jumps. It was my idea to write *Girls Who Sing Upside Down.* It was your idea to touch tongues.

We loved the other in each other. We loved each other without calling it love.

Was the break-up just part of our mysterious chemistry? Girl meets girl, they submerge in friendship too deep to untangle—until the untangling, without a way to weave themselves back together.

In my early twenties, I visited your dad to get some advice about a job I was considering in the film business. He was a very old man by then. *You're better than that,* he told me, *don't get involved in the movie business. It's not a nice business.* Your father had always spoken so fondly of his time in Hollywood making costumes for everyone from Rudolph Valentino to Jane Russell. When we were kids, you and I would jokingly ask him to call that director friend of his and have him put the two of us in a movie together. *Why not?* he'd say with a smile, but of course we were just kidding around. The movie business was his line of work, not something we wanted for ourselves.

I asked him what he meant by his anti-Hollywood remark. He told me that your mother had been an unknown movie actress and that the company she kept had been her undoing. He got custody, promising himself when you were a baby that he would keep you from her. *She never pulled herself out of the mess she made,* he said, *and I didn't want my daughter under her influence.*

You must have been told a version of your family history before we met. And your dad likely filled you in as you got older. It makes sense that you wouldn't have wanted to talk about it when we were young. And as we grew up, I guess we had more important things to think about than your mother.

I ended up taking the film job but worked only briefly in the not-nice business before developing other interests.

When you returned from the first of your many overseas travel adventures, my mom heard you were getting married and offered to throw you a bridal shower. You told her you weren't really into showers, but because it was her, you gratefully accepted. *I think of her as Mom,* you told me when we saw each other at the shower. You'd never actually said so, but it made sense. My mother adored you, and without putting words to it, you had adored her, too. At the shower, you told me that one of your most treasured memories was of being at our house on Mother's Day and bringing my mom breakfast in bed. I had no memory of it. It would have been just one more Mother's Day for me.

When your son called yesterday, I wasn't prepared. You and I had not been in contact much beyond birthday cards, neither of us ever forgetting the other's *day of earthly arrival,* as we aptly called it on your tenth birthday. We had met for dinner a few times over the last thirty years, but we were in our own spheres. As I followed your online postings, you inspired me with your wild journeys to every continent on Earth. There was beautiful you in Tanzania hiking to some treacherous peak; frozen California girl reveling and ice fishing in Greenland; righteously boozing it up with Irish comrades; dancing to the magic of the Aurora Borealis.

You traveled alone, leaving your less daring husband behind, falling in with fellow adventure-hustlers along the way. With summers off from your job, you didn't mind spending your modest income on getting you wherever you wanted to go. As soon as you returned from one far-flung jaunt you began planning the next one. I was never jealous. Comparing my humble exploits to yours was never the point. What thrilled you thrilled me.

The part of me that was us is still there. Although we weren't close as adults, spoke and socialized infrequently, it didn't matter. Because at seven, eight, nine, and ten through thirteen? We were as intimate as two humans could ever be. And that earliest bond doesn't break.

So, when your son asked me to visit you sooner rather than later, I rushed to you. You wanted me to be the last to see you. And while I was initially stunned by your request, it made sense. Of the many connections you had forged over a lifetime, ours needed to be the last. Because it was a clue. Because it was easy and true. Because it was the first.

Crow Boy & Ollie

Crow Boy & Ollie

Crow Boy

Hey, Bird Boy! You a spy?

The tallest kid, the one who most needs a shave above his upper lip, is shouting at me. I've seen him at the produce market with his sexy mom. Black-rimmed eyes, bright red lipstick, high heels with painted toes sticking out. All dressed up to buy vegetables.

Yeah…I'm spying on the crows.

He and his fellow students from the Persian Jewish school next to my bus stop are arriving for their before-school prayers, I'm clicking away, and they're pointing at me, laughing and mouthing off in Farsi. I know they think it's weird, me aiming my camera at the phone wires that stretch between their storefront school and a billboard showing a guy doing sit-ups at Crunch gym. These kids see me every morning and I'm always just waiting for the bus, no camera, no action. Now I'm twisting around trying to get the best angle and they think I'm nuts.

On one wire: eight crows lined up like fat soldiers, one loner at the opposite end. On another: four bunched up together, then a space, ten more together, another space, then twenty more. On a third: one oddball taking a whole wire to himself.

My school starts in forty-five minutes, the bus will be here in five, and I'm scrambling to shoot the birds. Why the wires anyway, instead of the big bushy trees along Pico? Maybe they get an electrical buzz.

You're crazy! Who cares about some dumb birds! another kid yells.

Pray for me, okay? I say.

Are you Jewish? the tall one asks.

Half.

Which half?

The crazy half.

The bus pulls up, and the Persian kids scream and wave at me as I get on. I flash them the peace sign through the window and feel a little jealous. Seems like they're having fun, all waving in the same goofy, kid-like way. Like they really belong together.

Ollie

Twenty-six, twenty-seven, twenty-eight, twenty-nine. At three-hundred and seventy-eight, it'll be the center of town. Numbers get me there every day. Prevents my mind from wandering down the damn tunnel. Fog shivering wet, gulls squawking in that bird language. Been here so long I can tell one voice from another. Insistent screecher. Big kahoona. High-pitched whiner. And silent champ— catching a wave of air, riding it all the way into town, the most like me. A hundred seventeen, a hundred eighteen, a hundred nineteen... up steep Chautauqua Boulevard. Impatient cars. Revving engines. Shrill honking. Faces avoiding me or staring too long. Farther up the hill. Velvet lawns, eucalyptus, mansions, barking dogs. Love the dogs. Especially this big wooly sheep dog like one I had as a kid. Used to follow me to the beach. Run with me into the waves, arms of almighty Pacific. A hundred ninety-eight, a hundred ninety-nine...

Ah, two hundred, my tree-lined alley. Let's see what the classy trash bin has to offer me today. Stub of a Subway sandwich. Half-full green bottle of beer? Soda? Take it for later. Now a quick piss without being noticed. Hey little scruffy cat, I see you behind the bin. Whatsa matter, pussy, never seen a beachcomber take a leak?

Crow Boy

It was Leonard Cohen who got me going on this whole crows-on-the-wire thing. Him and Passover. Every year my mom makes up her own *seder* using the basic Moses story but substituting haiku, editorials from the *LA Times,* and lyrics from her favorite songwriters. This year it was Leonard Cohen. She thinks *Let my people go* is somehow related to *Like a bird on a wire, like a drunk in a midnight choir, I have tried in my way to be free.*

I had walked to my bus stop hundreds of times, but Leonard's words made me look at the Pico Boulevard crows differently. I saw them getting tipsy up there on the wire, choosing a spot next to their buddies. Bunch of drunk birds singing on a wire in the middle of the night. As for trying to be free—if you're a bird, doesn't that mean flying away, not hanging out on a wire?

I wouldn't mind flying out of here. Away from L.A., from the people in my neighborhood who are too religious for their own good, from my parents who expect me to be another Moses or Leonard Cohen, even from my friends who are so freaked about getting into college they think they'll self-destruct if they're not accepted.

What if you don't picture yourself in college? What if you have other ideas for what you want to do with your life? I had a big fight with my dad about that last night. He thinks I'm making a big mistake not going along with the program. But one more semester, I'll be done with high school and I'm taking off. Travel around on my own. Get up when I want to, do whatever pops into my head, even if it's just shooting birds all day.

The bus is speeding along the Ten to the beach, but when it gets to Chautauqua and Coast Highway, two stops before Pali High, I see all these seagulls swirling around a clump of black dots in the ocean—surfers in their wetsuits—and I decide what the hell. I'm getting off. Skip school, get friendly with the birds, shoot some beach stuff. I've never ditched before, but it's about time I start thinking beyond the walls of school. Free as a bird.

Ollie

This hill never gets easier no matter how many mornings I climb it. Damn calves are hurting, dizzy-ass cars, seagulls trying to attack me. Drivers yelling at me to watch out or I'll get killed. No—Chautauqua is my road. Get to Sunset, I'll go to Irv's Deli, panhandle a bit. Get a bagel and cream cheese. And a beer. Two hundred fifty-three, two-hundred fifty-four...Turn and take a look at that ocean. White with glare. Little black bobbing dots—guys waiting for a big one. Me and Edmonds caught them. Walked with our boards down Chautauqua before we could drive. Edmonds bragging about feeling-up some stacked chick. Teasing me about French kissing that girl with braces. Heading to the waves that rode us into sweet oblivion.

Crow Boy

I run over to the other side of Coast Highway, then tromp through the sand to get closer to the water. The only people at the beach this morning are a few joggers and the small group of surfers paddling some pretty tame waves. It's still foggy, but the sun is making its slow way through it. I want some shots of the surfers and am hoping one of them will go for a wimpy wave to give me a vertical image. The black wetsuits will be good contrast against the pale ocean.

A surfer hops to his feet, knees bent, a decent wave coming up behind him. I'm shooting fast so I won't miss the action, not waiting to check out what I have before clicking the next one. I'm no surfer and don't know the fancy names they give all their moves, but the guy is crouching, twisting forward, doing the pivot thing with his feet until he stands inside the curling water and rides it all the way in. I snap about ten good shots.

Then I hear the crash. Metal on metal—like a small bomb.

Ollie

Traffic killing, jamming my ears, crushing metallic. Gone-wild solo drums. Surf-pounding god almighty. Where are you? I'm falling. Catch me, Edmonds. In your garage. Reverb baby. Ha! Someone is falling down drunk. It's your dad's Coors. It's me, I'm the drunk. I am the bad-ass drunk surfing drummer slamming down again.

Crow Boy

Within minutes the sirens are racing up Chautauqua and so am I. Flashing reds shoot through the misty air like giant sparklers. My backpack slows me down a little, but the adrenalin's pumping and I make it up the hill at the same time as the squad cars and ambulance. Honking commuters are trying to pull over to the right, scrunching around Chautauqua's curves. A yapping dog is going ballistic at the side of the road where the two cars have just collided—a Lexus 430 convertible and a Mercedes ML 350. Not much damage to either one, and the drivers are obviously unharmed enough to scream at each other full blast.

But then I see a skinny, middle-aged, blonde guy flattened out in the middle of the road. Blood all over his tan leathery face and arms, pants leg ripped open below the knee—lots of blood there too. I've never seen a person who's been run over. Did he just get knocked down, or did he fly into the air? The Lexus woman and Mercedes guy finally come over to check out how badly the guy is hurt and scribble insurance info on a piece of paper that they shove into his jacket. He's moaning so I know he isn't dead, and a policeman is asking him his name and other questions. Then the ambulance guys come over and move him onto a stretcher. He moans even worse. I am standing close enough to the guy so I can see his eyes are dark blue like wet ink. When he looks up at me, I take his picture.

Ollie

Buckling through the fog, leaping to his feet, quick bottom turn, twist inside it, curl-bend with it. Is that Edmonds riding it in with me? A kid with a camera crouching in front of me? Same wise eyes, curly brown hair. Fog getting thicker, whiter, mass of foam trailing us into shore. Edmonds' howling guitar fading in, fading out.

Crow Boy

Who're you? the cop asks me as they're bundling up the injured guy to get him ready to go. And then the guy says, barely loud enough to hear over all the commotion, *my buddy.* One eye flutters open and shut, which I'm pretty sure is him winking at me. Then both of his eyes close. As the paramedics give him a shot of something and shove him into the ambulance, I tell the cop, *He's a friend. I'm going with him.*

His eyes open halfway a few times as we speed down Coast Highway in the ambulance. When he looks at me, I try to reassure him. *Hey, it's gonna be alright, Oliver,* is all I can think to say. I'd heard the police say his name, Oliver Hunt, when they found an ID card in his jeans pocket. When we get to the hospital, I run alongside the stretcher and Oliver wakes up for a second, gives me that wink again. Maybe he thinks I'm someone else.

In the waiting room, I read an article in *People* about athletes on steroids and another about fallen heroes in Iraq only a few years older than me. Then I watch these two little kids rolling a rubber ball back and forth and snap a few pictures of them. Finally a pretty doctor who looks like one of the Persian kids' moms, walks out of the emergency room and calls out for Oliver Hunt's relative.

His leg is broken, she says. *Other than that, he's extremely fortunate. Are you his son?*

I look into her pretty black-outlined eyes and tell her I'm a distant relative. She says he'll be ready to leave as soon as he gets his crutches.

Ollie

Walking on damn crutches, left leg heavy with fat cast. Way harder than making it up Chautauqua. Curly haired kid getting up from orange plastic chair coming toward me. Do I know him? Why does he have that sorry-for-what-you've-been-through look on his face? Like Edmonds only taller. Where is Edmonds? Was he driving the crashing car? Is this kid related?

Crow Boy

I ask where he wants to go and tell him I'll help him get on a bus. He doesn't say anything, just shakes or nods his head. No, he doesn't have anyone he can stay with. No relatives, no friends. Yes, he is hungry, and yes, he wants to go back to the beach. *My home*, he says. I decide I'd better go with him.

I only have eight dollars, so after we get off the bus at Coast Highway, I help him hobble over to a hamburger stand stuck in the sand near the bike bath. I'm pretty hungry too and order us burgers and Cokes. We sit at one of the picnic tables, and I help him prop his leg up on the other bench. We eat our burgers but he doesn't say anything other than *Thanks, pal*, after we get our food. The silence between us is awkward at first, but the surf is kicking up and the crashing waves drown out our lack of conversation.

So what'd you do when you were younger? I finally ask. We have to shout to be heard over the waves.

Surfed…and played drums. His voice is like gravel, but friendly.

You were in a band? I shout back.

Me and Edmonds. I played drums, he was guitar.

Did you play out anywhere? I ask.

He nods his head, which is lit up by the reddish-orange sun going down behind him. He waits for the tide to roll back out in between crashes to answer me.

Yeah. Don was on bass. We played in Edmonds' garage, he shouts.

I want to ask him why he's homeless, what he'd done for a job before he got this way – but I figure it'd be rude. The way he's looking out at the blue-black ocean, it's like everything he wants and loves is out there.

I pick up my camera, and motion to him that I want to take his picture.

What for? he yells over the crashing.

It's what I do, I tell him.

Well then, do what you gotta do, he says.

Ollie

Guess the kid must be related to Edmonds – maybe his younger brother. Don't remember Edmonds having a younger brother but can't remember a lot of things. It's getting cold. Be hard to reach the rock palace before dark on these damn crutches. Nice of this kid to buy burgers. Funny kid - snapping pictures of me and the gulls picking at my French fries. Might as well ask him…*Feel like escorting me to my pad?*

Crow Boy

When he speaks it's like he's stuck in a time warp. Pad? Escorting me? It's late, and I know my parents will be worried, but I can't just leave him here. We walk along the bike path for about a quarter of a mile, me trying to walk slow enough to keep pace with his hobbling, and him stopping every few minutes to lean on me and rest. Fortunately, there aren't many bike-riders out tonight so we have the path pretty much to ourselves. When I give him my shoulder and hang on to his rib cage so he won't topple over, I can feel how bony his body is. I'm thin, but he borders on not being there at all. His matted, blonde-gray hair smells like seaweed and blood.

I finally ask how much farther we have to go, and he points toward a clump of jagged black rocks that are barely visible in the dark fog. *That's your pad?* I ask. He answers that it's been his address for thirty years.

Ollie

Kid takes off his backpack, lays it in the sand. Moves the guitar out of the way, grabs the blankets stuffed inside one of my boxes. Lays them out, helps me stretch out. Asks me how I like it here. Tell him the rock palace keeps the wind out pretty good. Asks if I play the guitar. Tell him I'm keeping it for a friend. I don't talk about Edmonds. Me and him didn't have to put it in words. Just knew we were brothers. Surfing brothers, rock 'n roll brothers. Celebrated our June birthdays after graduation...night surfing, plastered on rum and coke. Edmonds left for college, gave me his guitar, white Fender Stratocaster. *Keep it for me*, he said. *We'll jam when I come back.* Never happened. Couple times a day I pick up the Fender, air-strum it like Edmonds used to. Now the kid's fiddling with the guitar. His thwanging is pitiful, but in this faint light he looks the part.

Crow Boy

I help Ollie lie down on his dirty blankets and try to imagine how freezing he's going to be all night. I guess you get used to sleeping outdoors after thirty years, but now the poor guy has his broken leg to deal with. He doesn't seem to be bothered by any of it. We share a few stale Fig Newtons and lukewarm Sprites he has stashed inside one of his cartons. Then he asks if I've ever surfed, and I tell him I haven't but that I'd spent a few years on a skateboard and that was probably the same kind of feeling, without the ocean.

The ocean's the whole point, he says. *You're part of it when you know what you're doing.*

Then he rifles through an old backpack and pulls out a ripped-up snapshot of a blonde kid scrunched inside a curling wave, his arms outstretched like the wingspan of a half-human bird.

That's me at your age. Just starting to get the hang of it.

Looks like you were really good, I say.

One of the best.

He doesn't say it in a bragging way.

So how about you, kid? he asks. *I've got my ocean—what do you got?*

He has these saucer-shaped eyes that make him look like he's still an intense, curious kid. And now his curiosity and intensity are focused on me.

I guess I like taking odd pictures, I say. *Seeing things most people don't notice…or care about.*

He closes his eyes and nods, and his mouth twists into a half-smile.

Like these crazy thieving seagulls? he asks.

A couple gulls are picking at our cookie crumbs, and Ollie is waving them away.

Yeah, I say, *…and you.*

He nods and kind of stares me down with those flying saucer eyes again. Then he asks me to play the unplugged electric guitar some more.

It's not what I'd call playing, I say.

That's okay, he says, closing his eyes as I twang off-key for a few minutes. The waves are my back up, crashing rhythmically to help drown me out. I think I've put Ollie to sleep with my ragged playing, so I put down the guitar. But then he opens his eyes and reaches for it with both of his bony arms and puts it in my lap.

It's yours, he says, *Time I let it go anyway.*

I don't want the guitar, but I don't want to be rude. The old rusted instrument is the most valuable thing Ollie has, and I guess he wants to pay me back for helping him out. His only other possessions are his blankets, a few clothes, an old hibachi—and an ancient surfboard. So, I thank him and lie – tell him that, as a matter of fact, I have just started to teach myself guitar.

Then I say I have to get going, but that I'll come back and visit him sometime. He smiles and raises his shoulders, as if to say, *whatever.*

I know he doesn't expect me to come back.

I grab the guitar and my backpack, walk up to Coast Highway, and catch the bus back home.

After lying to my parents about where I've been, I go to my room and download the two photos of Ollie. In the first one he's splayed all bloody in the middle of Chautauqua, but there are rays of diffused daylight striking his head, almost like a crown of sun. The second is against the blue-black ocean at the hamburger stand. A close up. Ollie's eyes are blue saucers flying off to some unknown destination. Maybe I'll make an Ollie wall in my room. The two photos and the rusty guitar next to it, like a sculpture.

Outside, the full moon makes it seem like early morning. I want to try for the birds-on-a-wire again, so I grab my camera, sneak out the back door and run over to my favorite spot. I see five fat crows sitting on a wire at almost perfectly even intervals under the Crunch billboard. The light from the moon favors them. Maybe they sit there together because they're not sure where to fly next. Maybe they like to hang out with their friends before flying solo.

I snap the picture and know it will be a winner. But the one I really want to get is of the loner off to the side. The way the inky-blue neon sign glows around him, he looks like he is still part of the sky.

Tickets

Tickets

Playing deaf, Jasmine doesn't answer when a woman at the next station asks *how old is your baby?* Looking down at her as yet unpainted nails, she is not present. (Why would I speak of my baby with him in the room?)

Phil—fiftyish, alcoholic gut, too-tight jeans—bops around the nail salon showing off baby photos on his iPhone and answers for her: *Six weeks.*

Look at your body after only six weeks! Tonya says. *How do you do it, Jasmine? Are you sure you really had a baby?* Tonya giggles like she does when she tells one of her famous dirty jokes.

Jazzy still needs to lose ten pounds, Phil says. *She's lookin' hot again but she's gotta lose those few extra pounds. We'll do it though, won't we, honey?*

Jasmine says nothing. (I don't give a flaming shit for whatever comes from that mouth.)

So what color you want, Jasmine? Tonya's sister, Cam, takes one of the girl's hands in hers and checks out her nails. *Going somewhere special tonight?*

I'm taking her for a night on the town, Phil says. *Her mom's babysitting with Ethan. Black, right Jazzy?*

Jasmine nods without looking at him, her pert mouth unyielding. (So convenient that he loves to answer for me. Keep it up while you still can, big guy).

Black's good, Cam says. *Very trendy.*

You want me to do yours too, Phil? Tonya toys with him. *You'll look like a young stud with black nails and your sexy jeans!*

Maybe I should, huh? he says.

Where you taking Jasmine? Cam asks.

Taylor Swift concert, Staples Center. I got primo tickets from a big music producer I know. Backstage passes, the whole nine yards.

Jasmine sneers. (Nine yards, oh wow).

Hey Tonya, Phil pivots, *guess how much a mani-pedi is in Thailand?*

What—you had a mani over there but you won't have one here? Tonya teases. *You don't like me, Phil? Lori could paint you some black nails while Jasmine's getting hers done.*

Cam and Lori offer Phil flirty smiles.

Nah, thanks anyway. But really, guess how much it costs over there, Tonya?

She guesses: *Ten dollars? Probably more pricey than it used to be in Vietnam.*

Yeah, he says. *About ten. And that's in Bangkok. But you ladies make out pretty well here, huh?*

They work hard for it, says a white-haired woman getting her toes painted metallic blue. *Twelve hours a day.*

Phil turns to the woman, squints, resents having to acknowledge her.

Yes, they do, he says. Shoving the iPhone in his pocket, he takes a seat in the small waiting area and leafs through a *People*.

Hey Jasmine, Cam asks, *does Phil ever take you to the Thai Palace? A client told me the food is yummy.*

Phil looks up from his magazine. *She only eats Thai food her Mom makes. Right, Jazzy?*

Jasmine presses her rosy lips together, stabs him with the look.

You ever seen a picture of Jazzy's mom? Phil asks. *She's a fox too, especially for her age.*

Now he's up again slithering from station to station, showing everyone his iPhone photo of an attractive woman with shoulder length wavy hair and wide eyes that beg forgiveness. She is much younger than Phil, the guy who married her daughter.

Jasmine knows: (If anyone asked my mom—how could you, why did you allow this guy to poke his body into your young daughter—she would say it was our chance and the baby our prize.)

Phil strides over to the station where Jasmine is having her nails painted black. Pulls up a stool and puts his arm around her. *You know, I've traveled all over Asia. Singapore, Malaysia, Indonesia... never been to Vietnam, but Jazzy and her Mom? The sexiest and sweetest – bar none.*

Aww, that's so sweet, Cam says, looking up at Jasmine who refuses the bait.

It's true, Jazzy. I mean it, he says, kissing her on the cheek.

Hopping off the stool, he swings around to Tonya who engages him with her practiced charm.

You were lucky, Phil. Very lucky guy. You probably have one of those Chinese lucky cats in your bedroom, right? She winks at Jasmine but tries to puzzle it out: (How can this pretty teenager share her bed with a lizard? Does she hold her breath when the gecko comes at her? What does she use to numb the degradation?)

Tonya and Cam and Lori are unaware of Jasmine's special powers, perfected over the months that she's been sentenced to the old guy's bed. The lights go out and she vanishes, erases herself from his clutches and mind-flees back to the boy who was her love, her spirit. The boy with the bad luck to be born to the wrong family in the wrong country.

Jazzy's my lucky charm, Phil says. *My lucky kitty. Look what she gave me – this baby boy of mine.* He takes out his phone again and shows another photo to Tonya.

Looks just like you Phil, right Jasmine? Tonya winks.

Jasmine's mouth twists to kill. She looks down to admire her black mani and remembers her bargain: (I will unshackle and own my life. Soon. And it will be worth a million manis more than this free country and his lousy Taylor Swift tickets.)

Raw Pink

Raw Pink

Marsha lays out tomorrow's outfit at the foot of her bed. Minnie Mouse visor, Little Mermaid headband, Tinkerbell earrings, Chip 'n Dale necklace, Dumbo tank top, Daisy Duck zip-up sweatshirt, Goofy watch, Winnie the Pooh slacks, Princess Jasmine backpack, Pocahontas socks and Sleeping Beauty sneakers. Each item brings back a distinct thrill from her previous trips. And each is a favorite shade of pink—from blush to shocking.

It was a challenge selecting what to wear tomorrow from her vast Disneyland collection, as she owns over fifty articles of clothing, from jackets and pajamas to moccasins and flip-flops. Some of the shorts and slacks are a bit tight (she has gained a little weight over the years), but that doesn't really matter to Marsha. How she looks in the clothes isn't the point. When she is dressed in her special outfits during her twice-yearly escapes to Disneyland, a joyful essence flashes inside her and she feels in tune with the person she knows herself to be. The carefree whimsy of the animal characters and the innocent power of the fairytale princesses lifts Marsha out of the ordinary into a wonder-filled reality, although none of her friends or colleagues would ever understand that.

Marsha only wears the clothes from her collection when she visits Disneyland, and waiting for those dates to appear on her calendar is as pleasantly unbearable as the countdown to her dates with

Roger was so long ago. Now the minutes are slowly ticking off until tomorrow morning when she will finally put on her rainbow of pinks and board the plane to Orange County. She already senses the transcendent feeling that will overcome her tomorrow when she enters the magical haven she has been returning to in secret for more than three decades. Not one person knows where she spends her semi-annual vacations, and she enjoys creating her own private mystery.

*

Amber climbs into bed with the stuffed pony Kyle won for her at the Visalia carnival last summer. She knows it's a silly superstition, but she hopes the animal will bring her good luck. Tomorrow is another check-up, and Amber has to go alone. Her mom couldn't get off work, and Kyle couldn't miss another day of track. And with Marsha going on vacation, Amber is worried something might go wrong and she'll have no one to talk to. She clutches the pony to her chest and whispers in its ear: *Make this be over soon.*

*

Marsha can't fall asleep. The anticipation of tomorrow's trip and the stress of her final day before vacation has her keyed up. It was a chaotic day at work. She had spent all week tying loose ends and getting things in order for her assistant, who would be handling the caseload details. There was one client Marsha was especially concerned about—the Robeson's birth mother, Amber, who seemed to need Marsha's attention more than her other teenage birth moms. Initially Amber's endless need to check in with her had gotten on Marsha's nerves, but now she found herself looking forward to the girl's frequent calls. *I'm sorry to keep bothering you, Marsha*, and her cheery voice would belie her ongoing anxiety. Marsha enjoyed being able to reassure Amber that everything would turn out just fine. She wasn't sure why, but the girl meant more to Marsha than the others. Sure, the angry rapper music she played on that contraption she plugged into her ear and the low-cut t-shirts she wore to her appointments with the Robesons weren't exactly appropriate. Not to mention getting pregnant at fifteen. But maybe none of this is Amber's fault. Girls like Amber don't have the solid upbringing Marsha had. Maybe the cleavage and brutal-sounding music compensate for Amber's lack of educational and professional focus.

Marsha had been focused for as long as she could remember. She had gone to Berkeley in the late sixties, but whenever she told anyone this, she had to follow it up with *not everyone who went to Berkeley was a protester*. In fact, Marsha was a member of the Campus Committee to Support Our Troops and had organized their campaign to send Christmas cards to the guys overseas. She wore tailored skirts and crisp white blouses, and even though she majored in sociology and later became a social worker, her values had always been slightly conservative. In her senior year her boyfriend Roger was sent to Vietnam. They had been dating for two years and Marsha had known this was coming. An ROTC enlistee, he could have taken a student deferment but Roger wanted to serve. Marsha was proud of him and made the decision to lose her virginity the night before he left for training camp.

Roger splurged and they spent their last night together at the Claremont Hotel atop one of Berkeley's most spectacular hills. The view from their room was of the entire glittering Bay, the spires of San Francisco, and the Golden Gate Bridge. Roger brought champagne and fancy chocolates, and they ordered in filet mignon dinners from room service. They danced to the soft ballads playing on the hotel radio, and then Roger made love to Marsha slowly and deeply, each kiss and each murmur fulfilling Marsha's childhood dream of merging with the perfect man, the one who would see beyond her beauty and her brains into her heart. Who would touch her with the same sweetness and strength that she carried inside herself.

In Roger's absence Marsha had finished her master's degree in social work. When the war crushed her hopes for a future with Roger, she eventually began to date a little. But she never found anyone as upstanding or as authentically a gentleman as Roger had been. Men seemed to change after the women's movement and the whole hippie thing. They were less sure of themselves yet pumped up on bravado and an immature pride in their bad manners. As if their looseness of character could cover up the fact that they didn't know how to be real men.

Marsha returned to her hometown in the San Joaquin valley and got a job with the adoption agency. She reasoned that in a more perfect world babies wouldn't need to be adopted, but she felt good about doing her part to place them in loving homes. Still, after living in the Bay Area and her relationship with Roger, Visalia left her yearning for something more. It wasn't that she was bored; she had meaningful work, friends at the agency, and season tickets to the Visalia symphony. And she wasn't a prude, but the men she had occasional dinner dates with never inspired even the slightest lustful twinge. Marsha craved a certain controlled ecstasy and the twice-yearly trips to Disneyland, which she had been taking now for over thirty years, filled that need. The past and future lands that were so scrupulously portrayed down to the last detail transported her beyond the everyday, the way Roger once had when he swirled her in his arms to Mantovani's violins.

Marsha isn't sure whether Disneyland makes her forget Roger temporarily or remember him more painfully, but now for a few sweet moments, he slips into her vision of a pink castle and dark jungle.

*

Amber dresses for her doctor's appointment, pulling the purple paisley t-shirt over her growing bump. Rifling through her box of eye-shadows, she finds a lavender wand and applies it to her pale lids, smiling at herself half-heartedly in the mirror. *I'm no Jennifer Anniston, but I'll get my body back. Marsha said so.* Her smile widens as she thinks of the woman who always seems to know what to say to make Amber relax just a little.

*

Marsha is used to the stares, pointed fingers, giggles, and rude comments when she wears one of her cherished outfits to Disneyland. So, when a teenage girl in short shorts and purple-streaked hair whispers to her friend loud enough for Marsha to hear, *Oh my god, look at that woman, she looks like a super-sized six-year-old,* Marsha doesn't flinch. A portly dad holding the hand of his jumpy little boy smiles at her. *Love your sweatshirt. My daughter has one exactly like it in bright yellow.* Marsha looks behind him in the ticket line at the sunburned, uncomplaining woman who is obviously his wife. She's holding a whimpering baby as well as the hand of a little girl eating a pop tart and getting the red oozy filling all over her face. *Thanks,* Marsha says. *It's one of my favorites.*

When You Wish Upon a Star plays throughout the ticket booth area, and Marsha remembers her first visit to Disneyland. She was seven and it was the happiest day of her life up until then, but also the most melancholy. She had never walked into a world that so fulfilled her innermost seven-year-old yearnings, that so indelibly imprinted its perfected fantasies onto her developing brain. But she had never been so disenchanted either. On that first visit, what she had most looked forward to was entering the castle, the one with the swans floating all around it in bright blue water and the lovely princess-voice singing softly from inside the wishing well, as if the song was borrowed from Marsha's very own dream. It was the only wishing well she had ever seen, but she felt it was part of her inner landscape, the recorded voice singing to her alone. Marsha had begged her parents to wait until the end of the day to go inside the castle because she wanted to save the best for last, the way she always ate her yellow birthday cake first before savoring the creamy swirls of chocolate frosting. Tired from a full day at the park, filled with ice cream bars and hot dogs and lemonade, Marsha had held her mother's hand as they walked up the drawbridge to the castle, lit up with twinkling lights and enhanced by the dreamy voice of the princess wishing well. But to young Marsha's great disappointment, the inside of the castle never materialized. It wasn't there. Once she and her mother crossed through the portal, they weren't inside a castle at all. Instead, there was a fancy merry-go-round, a hat shop with strange mirrors and funny hats, and dozens of whizzing rides. There was no inside to the castle. It was only a shell.

Over the years Marsha had learned to gloss over those parts of Disneyland that had disillusioned her as a child. The castle, Toad's Wild Ride (where she'd glimpsed a workman beside the tracks in the dark), the Indians waving from the Riverboat shores (they looked too stiff to be real people). Yet even now, gazing down the crowded Main Street boulevard toward the silvery pink towers of Fantasyland, the castle still holds her in its spell.

*

Amber knows Marsha is on vacation for a few days and will only be available for emergencies. And maybe there's no need to bother her because the Robesons might not even care. Her contract with the agency specifies that the doctor will inform the Robesons of any irregularities discovered on the sonogram. And the doctor assured Amber that with the proper treatment, it could probably be fixed. So, doesn't that mean it isn't really a deformity? Besides, the Robesons are so anxious to have a baby – would they really mind, even if they do find out? With all the abnormalities babies can be born with, this isn't such a big deal, is it? As if offering a response, the baby kicks her with such force that Amber nearly loses her balance as she texts Marsha: *Worried they might not want the baby now!*

*

Marsha loves the old-fashioned street that's the first world you enter when you pass through the gates of the park. How many times has she wished that she could actually live on this street? Where the horse-drawn carriages and early model motor cars make time slow down so that you can appreciate the lace-curtained shop windows displaying their glass figurines, cuckoo clocks, silhouette portraits, and pointy lace up shoes. A barbershop quartet harmonizes on the patio of the red and white striped ice cream parlor, each singer genuinely happy to be performing for customers enjoying their sundaes and ice cream sodas. Flowers in brilliant primary colors are perfectly tended in the town square. And wouldn't it be wonderful to do all your shopping in the little dry goods store attended by the smiling clerks in spotless white aprons, the men sporting bow ties, the women wearing calico bonnets? Marsha has the ability to blot out the hordes of tourists that swarm through this section of the park like crazed bees, anxious to beat their way to the thrill rides she cares less about. As she walks slowly down the boulevard of yesteryear (she loves that word), she becomes a citizen of the 1890s, a woman in a long dress, a bustle and a bonnet...and a sunny song in her heart.

*

Driving to the mall where she plans to buy some paisley flip-flops to match her t-shirt, Amber can't stop worrying. It isn't like Marsha not to get back to her right away, even if she's on vacation. She's such a nice lady, smart, probably pretty when she was younger, but the thing Amber likes most about her is that she always does what she says she's going to do. Calls you when she says she will, is ready for you on the dot of your appointment time. Amber also likes that Marsha remembers your story and asks you questions that show she cares about you. Like *How do you and Kyle feel about giving up your baby?* She's nothing like Amber's mother, who has to be reminded of Amber's boyfriend's name and has never asked Amber one question about how Kyle feels about anything. And her mom never refers to the baby as *your baby*. When she mentions it at all, she just says, *the pregnancy*.

Maybe that's better anyway. Amber has pretty much come to think about the baby as the Robesons' child that she's having for them. She knows it will be cute because it will probably have soft blonde curls like Kyle and hopefully his straight nose and small ears. She can't put her own face onto the baby at all. But now with the defect, she's worried that it's somehow her fault. Maybe it's those weird vitamins she sent away for that are supposed to help you tone your body. It was before she had found out she was pregnant and she wanted to look hot in her new low-slung capris, but maybe the vitamins stayed inside of her and had a strange effect. Maybe instead of

in the land of glare

toning her body they had somehow congealed into the round clump at the end of the Robeson baby's little leg.

*

Placing the horn-like receiver into its cradle after listening in on a party line telephone in the Main Street general store, Marsha feels the coincidental vibration of her cell phone intruding on her trip back in time. Probably just her assistant unable to access a file. The old-fashioned wind-up phones are so much more fun, she muses, as she makes her way to a bench in the flower-filled Main Street town square. Smiling flirtatiously at the handsome young man driving a sputtering open-air motor car, Marsha can't help but remember Roger. They had never been to Disneyland together, as their romance occurred long before Marsha's obsession with the park, but he would have fit right in on Main Street—gentlemanly and hearty. She looks around at the perfectly replicated nineteenth century lampposts, the dazzling yellow and red chrysanthemums neatly arranged into the shapes of Jiminy Cricket and Pinocchio, the wide-eyed toddler cautiously shaking hands with a larger-than-human-sized, floppy-eared Goofy. Life should be like this, Marsha tells herself. This is the way people were intended to live. Convivial and open-hearted and surrounded by beauty. But somehow humans keep veering further and further off track.

*

Gunfire cracks through the air as the jungle boat captain shoots the alligator between the eyes. Marsha screams with her fellow travelers, delights to the Amazonian waterfall splashing her face, but is again annoyed by her pulsating cell phone. Taking it from her purse and throwing it into her backpack without checking its message, she whispers *Leave me alone*. The annoying device is a link to her professional self, which she wants to forget for the next seventy-two hours. *I'm entitled to these few days of escape, aren't I?*

As a little girl Marsha had learned which park attractions were the most reliably beguiling, which self-contained worlds would completely envelop her. The dark cruise through the jungle where wiggly hippo ears and twisting eyes bubbled up out of the menacing Amazon waters. The miniature highway where she could put her foot on a child-sized gas pedal and drive an almost-real sports car past believable little billboards. The cowboy saloon where high swinging doors opened onto a frontier-era barroom, complete with sawdust floor and a colorful stage of can-can dancers kicking mesh-stockinged legs to the player piano's rousing tunes while you drank root beer from real beer mugs. As a child Marsha had wanted to lose herself in such exotic settings, and as an adult she retains that longing. *And now, ladies and gentlemen*, the jungle boat captain proclaims, in a message Marsha has heard dozens of times but which still tickles her, *back to civilization and the most dangerous creatures of all: women drivers*.

*

Amber doesn't understand why Marsha is ignoring her. Maybe she's snorkeling or water rafting or something—she hadn't mentioned where she was going on her vacation. But Amber really needs to get Marsha's opinion on what she should do about the baby. She lays on her bed trying to watch TV and do her homework, but she can't concentrate. She goes over the situation once more in her mind so she's prepared to ask the questions intelligently when Marsha gets back to her. The Robesons selected her because she's in perfect health and has coloring and features similar to Mrs. Robeson. They had been sweet to Amber the few times they'd met, assuring her they would give the baby all the love and security the baby deserves. But what will they do if they find out that the baby inside Amber's stomach is not the baby they signed up for? That it's growing something strange at the end of its leg?

*

As a child, Marsha loved taking the river raft to Tom Sawyer's Island. All these years later, she again stands on the wood-planked raft with the other passengers crossing the "Mississippi" to the free-wheeling, play-by-your-own-rules kids' island. They're about to enter a world where you're free to run around like a wild Indian, explore and get lost and even be righteously scared. Marsha has never been afraid of much, either as a child or an adult. She grew up in a pleasant Visalia neighborhood with sensible parents who raised her to believe in her ability to face whatever challenges came her way. Their community was mostly inhabited by people they could trust, so Marsha's parents allowed her to go off all day during the summer and on weekends and create her own fun with her neighborhood pals.

As an adult, Marsha felt protected from most external threats. She lived in a security building and had never been afraid of break-ins or rapists. But she enjoyed the moderate doses of controlled fear that Disneyland provided. Now, inside a kid-sized dark cave, a skull and crossbones had been drawn and "One-eyed Pete was here!" had been scrawled by river rogues who threatened to kidnap or disfigure whoever dared confront them. Marsha had to crouch down to make her way through the opening, bumping into two scrawny kids. The smaller one was feeling his way through the dark with one hand and pulling on the older kid's t-shirt with the other. She followed so closely behind the two that she could smell the boy-sweat at the back of the smaller one's neck.

*

It was the name the doctor had given to the condition that left Amber with a freaky mental image. She pictures a baby's shortened leg with a hideous wooden foot resembling the bottom of a golf club, the fat round kind. She did a Google search and found a photo of an infant lying on his back, as if he was squirming to try to untangle his little foot out of its apparent L-shape. Even though the doctor explained that with braces and casts the child's condition could probably be corrected, Amber can't stop telling herself that she is producing a defective product. She wouldn't want to keep a baby who was defective, as sorry as she might feel for it or as blond and curly as its hair might be. She just has to pray that the Robesons won't mind. Studying the online photo of the wriggling baby, Amber has second thoughts about giving up her child if it turns out the Robesons don't want it. Maybe she *does* have it in her to be a good mother, even to a deformed baby. None of this is the baby's fault, after all; not the deformity and not having two tenth graders as birth parents. She and Kyle like hanging out and having sex, but could they really be parents? Amber desperately needs to talk to Marsha.

*

Marsha hears the riverboat band playing *Way Down Upon the Swanee River* as the distant paddle wheel propels the massive craft around the island for its last go-round. Still on the island, she sits on a rough wooden bench and munches on the popcorn she had stashed in her tote bag earlier in the day. Closing her eyes, she listens to the nostalgic tune that reminds her of her parents, her own "old folks" now long gone. They had brought her to this Disneyland nearly every summer when she was a child, probably imagining that she would bring her own children one day, but Marsha had long ago given up that fantasy. Still, she can't help but calculate how old her never-born children would be if she'd had them with Roger. Way too old to be romping around this wonderful island. Old enough to have their own kids. Slowly opening her eyes, Marsha sees the lights twinkling on the historic riverboat's decorative arches, against the navy-blue twilight darkening the island sky.

She wishes she could live forever in the loveliness of this finite world. In the distance she hears the last children laughing and screaming as they stumble across the wobbly bridge created from giant wooden barrels. The river raft captains call *all aboard* for the last trips back to the mainland. Marsha will get up in a second but allows herself a final moment of solitary bliss. She closes her eyes again and what flashes through her mind is the day she and Roger had gone hiking in Marin County a few weeks before he left for the base. She had marveled at how nimbly he sprinted up the steep wooded trail as if he had always lived on a mountain rather than the Wisconsin flatlands where he'd grown up. He was wearing his khaki shorts and she could see the muscles in his tanned calves, stretched and strong. *Were you a mountain goat in your last life?* she had shouted up to him. He turned around, his cheeks ruddy from the climb, his smile open and full. *A mountain goat in love with a cute auburn-haired goat-girl.* He ran back down to grab her and they had fallen, scraping a knee and an elbow, laughing at their irrepressible happiness.

Opening her eyes to the yellowing Frontierland lights across the river, a boy of about ten who might have been Tom Sawyer himself and a younger kid running after him dash past Marsha, brushing against a nearby clump of prickly bushes and darting into the small cave she had explored earlier. She hears their young voices echoing from inside the cave. *We can hide out here until the park closes! We'll have the whole island to ourselves,* the older one says. *But Dad said to meet them at the town square,* the young voice says. *Hey—I thought you wanted to go for a swim,* says the older boy.

Hearing the last island fun-seekers shuffling onto the Huck Finn river rafts headed back to the mainland, Marsha decides she will not be among them. The boys in the cave have sparked a challenge. A swim in the river? It isn't something she has ever dreamed of, but she *has* wished she could have free reign of the island, without the crowds and real world intrusions. Just her in the land of Huck and Tom—free to drift into their story. She'll hide out with the boys. Maybe even wade in the Mississippi.

She sees the boys run down to the water's edge, but they don't notice her sitting on the log bench behind the bushes. As she watches them throwing off their sneakers and wading into the river, she feels her cell phone vibrating through her tote bag. Relenting, she sees Amber's text: *Worried they won't want my baby. Call me!* She will call the girl in the morning. Amber is a sweetheart, but a worrier, and Marsha will assure her everything will be okay. For now, even Amber—Marsha's favorite kid having a kid—seems a distant reality.

Pulling off her socks and sneakers, Marsha walks down a dirt path to the river. She feels the stab of small rocks sharp against the soles of her feet but doesn't mind. Ankle-deep in the murky water, she suddenly hears the younger boy shrieking and the older one shouting, *Hold on! Darren! Hold on!* Rushing towards them in the dark, Marsha can barely see the two boys as their screams intensify. The brown water is much shallower than she had thought, but the littler boy is screaming so desperately that Marsha has a hard time grabbing him around his small bony chest. The older one is yelling in his highest voice *Darren cut his leg! It's not my fault!*

Marsha carries Darren up the embankment, but when she tries to lay him down, he screams even louder and won't let go of her. His small arms smelling of oily water latch on tightly around her neck as he sobs in pain. He has a deep, vertical gash nearly the entire length of his calf and it's gushing blood. *It wasn't my fault!* the older boy keeps repeating. At least he's crying now instead of screaming. Tying her sweatshirt tightly around the small, thin leg, Marsha asks the older boy how Darren got cut so badly. *On the track that goes under the water.* Marsha hadn't realized that the riverboat was on a track. She holds Darren on her lap and tells the older boy to help her scream for help.

It doesn't take long. After only about sixty seconds of screaming, *Help! We're on the island!* a motor boat, completely out of keeping with the frontier-era theme, comes to Marsha and the boys' rescue. When they get out of the boat, drenched and shivering, Marsha still holding the smaller boy in her arms, the three are escorted in a golf cart-like vehicle by two security officials through the backside of the park. They drive behind the cowboy saloon, the jungle boat ride, the castle and storybook village, and the old-time boulevard. Marsha feels a deep sadness as she witnesses the cracked hippo heads, fake covered wagon parts, poufy princess dresses, and all manner of pulleys and gears and machinery stored behind the structures she has spent so many years daydreaming about. She had always known the lands weren't real, but everything—almost everything, aside from the pink castle—had been so believable that it hurt her to witness the banal trickery that props up those entrancing worlds. And her heart sinks as she watches one of the young dry goods store clerks whipping a calico bonnet across the snickering face of a de-headed Pluto, shouting *I'm no 'ho, you fucking pervert!*

When they pull up to the office, Marsha carries Darren into the arms of his anxious parents. The Daisy Duck sweatshirt wrapped around his leg is soaked through with the boy's blood, which has also badly stained Marsha's tank top. The oily river scent clings to her wet clothes, but the instant she hands Darren over she misses his small trembling body. In the past half hour, it has made her own seem more vital. As the medical team attends to the boy, the park's chief security officer reaches out to shake Marsha's hand. *You're a real hero, ma'am,* he says.

Marsha is glad she remembered her first aid skills from the long-ago summer when she had volunteered at Cal Camp in Berkeley. But she knows she is not a hero.

*

Around midnight, Amber finally gives up hearing back from Marsha. She thinks about talking to her mother about the baby's condition but realizes her mom has never been someone to think things through from the other person's point of view, which is what Amber appreciates about Marsha. Marsha would probably tell her *If the Robesons decide not to adopt your baby, think of your child's best interests, Amber. If you were the baby and had the choice, what kind of home would you want to live in?* This was the question Marsha had posed to Amber after she first found out she was pregnant and her mother made the appointment at the agency. The question was simple, but it made sense. Amber realizes that she can now ask herself that question.

*

In the Disneyland Hotel that night, Marsha finds herself longing for Roger more intensely than she ever has. He was the only hero she has ever known. Unlike the blustering movie heroes who never lost their self-important swagger no matter how many body parts flew across the screen, Roger trained and fought and sacrificed selflessly. He was in it solely to do the right thing, the honorable thing.

Unlike the few men with whom she'd later had brief encounters, who mistook her lush red hair and curvaceous figure for a brash invitation, Roger knew how to make her feel like a lady, an intelligent princess. And how had she ultimately shown him her love and admiration?

She had visited Roger in the Oakland army hospital when he returned six months after their night at the Claremont Hotel, both legs blown off below his knees. The stumps were all she could focus on as she walked down the long line of soldier-filled beds to where he lay. She tried to quickly raise her eyes to meet his, but she spent too long staring at his stumps. As she bent down to kiss him, his lips were closed and hardened. Pulling her face away from his, still bent over his shortened body in a half-hearted embrace, she felt his raw pink stumps kicking against the mattress like impotent little fists.

A few months later, Roger was released from the hospital and rented an apartment in Berkeley not far from Marsha's. She wanted to love and marry him anyway, but she couldn't make herself give up the old Roger for the new one. As hard as she tried to convince herself that he was the same person who had been her mountain man, her suave dancer, her gentleman prince, he just didn't seem like Roger anymore. He left the Bay Area to return to his home in Viroqua, Wisconsin, and Marsha answered only the first of his several gloomy letters. *I know you, Roger,* she wrote, *and you're not a quitter. You'll get through this.* Although she knew she couldn't find it in herself to be with him anymore, Marsha would be faithful and hold the old Roger in her heart forever. But the shame would never leave her.

After a room-service breakfast of mouse-eared pancakes the following morning, Marsha finally returns Amber's call. Amber tells her about the baby's condition, and Marsha assures her that she will contact the Robesons and get their decision as soon as possible. Marsha hears Amber's faint whimper on the other end of the phone and feels a pull toward the teenager and her unborn child, as if they mean more to her than she can grasp.

Do you think they'll still want my baby? Amber asks. Marsha wishes Amber was there so she could make her believe that what she is about to say is the truth, not a cruel fantasy.

Who wouldn't want your baby? Marsha says. *Who wouldn't want your perfect child?*

A Boyfriend History in 10 Flavors

A Boyfriend History in 10 Flavors

1. Fire Balls

Popping a Fire Ball in your mouth was proof you were tough enough to stand the pain, to scorch your mouth without flinching. Hotter than cinnamon Red Hots, Fire Balls were dangerous candy. Bleeker bought them for me in sixth grade during lunch. He had faked a lunch pass to leave school and bought them at the candy store a few blocks away. So he not only risked getting caught for pulling off the lunch pass scheme, but for bringing the contraband candy onto the playground. And I risked sucking it. They were so huge you couldn't just quickly suck and swallow – the suck took forever. I didn't really like Bleeker that much—his white-blonde hair was too pale and his teeth too buck—but his nerve impressed me. And while it would be decades before I understood the layers of metaphor inherent in his gift of fiery sugar, I knew enough to appreciate the suck.

2. Spearmint Thin

Our routine was Eddie's design, not mine: weekends we'd go to Goody-Goody's for dinner, then drive up to Mulholland and make out until almost ten when I had to be home. Goody-Goody's was a drive-in coffee shop where the waitresses came to your car and clipped those heavy metal trays to the car window with your order. Eddie always ordered a cheeseburger, fries, milkshake, and the special Goody-Goody "the works" dessert – a thick slice of angel food cake, two scoops of vanilla ice cream, and oozing hot fudge poured over the whole thing. I always had a grilled cheese, fries, and a shake. After we ate and Eddie paid for our food, he would take out a stick of Wrigley's spearmint gum and fold it into his mouth. When he chewed, it made his lips look even thinner, and they were too thin already. I hated that gum. I tasted it when we made out, and it wasn't so much the dying mint flavor as the reminder of his too thin lips and his tight anxious routine. He suffered when I went away to college, tried to talk me into a campus closer to home. But I couldn't wait to get away from everything familiar, including those tentative spearmint lips.

3. Thousand Island

I begged him. Please let me go with you this time. Paul didn't like to be held back by a girl when he hitchhiked. You'd cramp my style, he'd say. I'd have to worry about you all the time. Besides, hitchhiking is an art. You have to chat up your rides, make them feel comfortable so they don't think you're some ax murderer or something. But he finally gave in when he realized I'd be an asset. I had an innocent look that would attract rides – we'd come across as two clean-cut college kids trying to make it back home to see our folks. Which was not what we were doing at all, though the college kid part was true. Paul's overall objective was to drive through every single state so he could scratch the U.S. off his to-do list. He'd already traveled through Turkey, Pakistan, Morocco, Brazil, and other exotic places, and the states were just a mundane continent he had to get out of the way. Our trip would be to Daytona Beach, so he could hit a bunch of southern states and we could say we'd done the spring fling thing, although we'd only be there one night and then have to turn around and come back to California.

On the road I had to abide by his rules, and there was one unbreakable one when it came to food: Breakfast, lunch, or dinner, I was to order only coffee and French fries, and ask the waitress to bring Thousand Island dressing for the fries. The point was: cost-effectiveness. Fries and Thousand Island fill you up. The perfect meal, Paul said. He was so cheap. His dad was an oil exec, and I knew he could have afforded a burger now and then. But I ate the fries with Thousand Island, grateful for the chance to see the world – or at least Arizona, New Mexico, Texas, Louisiana, Mississippi, Alabama, Georgia, and Florida from the back seat of a car. I wondered if the Brazilian version of fries and gloppy dressing would still make me crave a more generous boyfriend.

4. Rosewater

He cut a stunning figure sauntering across campus. Smoky olive skin, sleek black hair, and a lean, fit body set off by his elegant European clothes. For weeks we exchanged "the look" whenever we walked past each other: I see into you, you tempt me. He made his move at the Telegraph Avenue coffee house I frequented every night with my sister. May I buy you beautiful ladies a coffee? My sister rolled her eyes, I looked into his and nodded yes—to the coffee and anything else he might offer. He was from Saudi Arabia, here on a student visa getting his engineering degree. I loved the sound of the words: Saudi Arabia. On our first date he took me to the city to one of San Francisco's most posh restaurants. At nineteen, I had never had Middle Eastern food: couscous with slivered almonds and currants, succulent leg of lamb, sesame seed flat bread fresh from the oven. Dessert was the strangest: a confection of meringue, pistachio nuts, and rosewater. Is it really made from roses? I asked Malik. Instead of answering he put his arm around me and gave a slight squeeze to my shoulder. It was our first moment of touch. I loved his long dark fingers and his finesse. His look: you are sweet; naïve but sweet and lovely.

Our first and only night together was rosewater sweet. As it happened, however, the day following our night in the city the Middle East erupted in what would later be referred to as the Six-Day War. When my sister and I entered the coffee house, a group of Arab students, including Malik, was sitting together at a table in the corner. I couldn't understand why he didn't come over to our table, why his eyes avoided mine. Don't you get it, my sister said, you were just his Jewish conquest.

I confess to political and culinary naiveté. But I had tasted rosewater with an open heart.

5. Artichokes & Crème de Cassis

It was my first job out of college. In that time before the full flowering of women's opportunities, I had grabbed mine. I was doing interesting work and my boss was a man who respected my intelligence and creative bent. I had my share of self-doubt, but Stewart bolstered my confidence. You'll be fine. You can handle it. You're smart. He was fatherly but respectful, like a coach with his Olympic athlete.

Our ten-year age difference seemed vast to me, not to him. It was lunch – our daily lunches at the small French restaurant across the street from our office – that bridged the gap. I don't know how we happened to choose the same menu item the first time we had lunch together, but it was what we both wanted: artichoke vinaigrette. Nothing else; the huge flowery plant was our whole meal. Growing up in California I knew artichokes. My mom served them with melted butter or mayonnaise. Dipping and eating them leaf by leaf, scraping off the delicate green flesh with your bottom teeth: it was a unique mealtime experience. Not remotely related to "eating your vegetables." Stewart introduced me to the aperitif we always had with our artichoke lunch. You'll like it. It's sweet but not too sweet. Crème de Cassis, made from crushed blackcurrants and poured over ice.

A slight buzz at the end of the meal made the afternoon's work more agreeable—and my attraction to Stewart unavoidable. I couldn't help it. I knew he was married with two little kids, but I somehow pushed them and their mother out of sight. Stewart was handsome and suave, sharp and funny, but I don't think I realized then what I found most attractive: he was doing with me what my father was doing with countless women. Cheating. I was outrageously angry at my father. After twenty-seven years of marriage to my mother, who adored him, he left her—probably because he hadn't had his fill of bad girls before he married my good girl mom. I was filled with rage, and Mr. Crème de Cassis allowed me to engage in an unconscious dance: I'll let you fall for me and cheat on your wife, and then I'll get back at you and my father: I'll leave you, hurt you. Which is not to say I hadn't fallen hard for Stewart: I still can't eat an artichoke without a glass of blackcurrants, crushed and liquefied.

6. Refried Beans

Singers, guitar players, piano players—all they had to do was play or sing passionately well, and I was in love. Looks, formal education, kindness: not necessary if the music rang true. I had this notion that the guy *was* his music. Soulful music equaled soulful guy. If he was socially awkward or insensitive or dismissive of me, I chalked it up to artistic temperament. Musical output was what counted and just being around an accomplished musician fulfilled a deep yearning. What I didn't get until my late twenties, when I started writing songs and performing, was that my boyfriend musicians were stand-ins for me. I wanted what they had and rather than work to get there, I hung around them hoping I'd receive creative gratification by osmosis.

Jess was a mandolin player, a messenger of the angelic strings. Bluegrass, jazz, old-timey—his fingers flew in service of the holy tones only a mandolin can deliver. I was mad for that mandolin. Jess? He had zero personality, pasty skin, and a number of unmentionable bad hygiene quirks. But, oh, that mandolin. And in addition to bringing me to the gates of mandolin heaven, Jess enlightened me on the simple beauty of a food I had only eaten occasionally in Mexican restaurants: refried beans. At that time this unpretentious staple was not as ubiquitous on gringo supermarket shelves as it is today. I had never heard of eating refried beans unless they appeared on your plate at El Cholo or on Olvera Street alongside cheesy enchiladas and Spanish rice. And I should mention that Jess was Jewish, not Mexican. They're tasty and easy, he said, bringing our dinner to a simmer and slitting open the package of tortillas with his teeth. I had always loved beans of any kind: lima, baked, garbanzo. And refried? Who would have thought you could eat them in the privacy of your own home. I didn't stick with Jess that long. But he played a mean mandolin on my first demo. It still rocks.

7. French Roast

Russ was more like a girlfriend than a boyfriend. We could talk about anything. He was a good listener when I had a problem and knew when not to give advice. He also loved gossiping about which local politician or professor had skeletons in their closet. He was brilliant and inspiring, joyful and socially conscious. He volunteered at a shelter on skid row. Read Roland Barthes, Gore Vidal, Germaine Greer. Introduced me to Japanese erotic art and Raymond Chandler novels. His most lasting influence: he taught me how to brew the perfect cup of coffee.

I was almost thirty before I became a coffee lover. As a kid, the few times I took sips of my parents' Yuban I thought coffee tasted like dishwater. And on my nightly ventures to the Berkeley coffee house where I'd met the Saudi Arabian, I ordered Café Mocha with whipped cream – the chocolate and cream obliterating the taste of coffee. But now I wanted to learn to make coffee like Russ, whose brew ushered in a beloved habit I never wanted to break. You start with quality beans, he said, dark, greasy, aromatic. Use a good machine to grind them, don't go cheap. Scoop enough coffee into the cone filter of your Melitta to create full-bodied strength. Boil a kettle of water. And then the step most people ignore: at first, pour only enough water to dampen the ground coffee. Then pour the boiling water little by little until the pot fills. Don't overwhelm the ground beans; let coffee take its time. He was right. The richest things in life can take time. Russ and I gave our friendship time to percolate into something more. We kissed and fooled around a little, but we both had to finally face the fact that Russ was gay. He eventually found love with the proper gender, and I found bliss in a cup.

8. Sunflower Seeds

Che Guevara was sitting at a table near the tiny stage where I sang. A Sephardic Jewish Che in a denim shirt. I finished my set and walked to the bar where a scarlet drink awaited me. Compliments of the hunk with the mustache, Ellie said. I took a sip of cranberry juice, no vodka, then walked over to thank him. You seem like a cranberry girl—sorry, woman. Girl's okay, I said. I like your songs, they're enigmatic, he said. Then asked me more questions about myself than any man I'd ever met. When the conversation finally turned to him, I learned he was getting his Ph.D. in history and ran six miles a day. At thirty-one, I was juggling a so-so day job, the singing gig, and another rocky relationship. Did I need this gentle scholar to complicate my life? Turns out I did. After too many years of flitting from one angst-ridden romance to another (was I still trying to sort out the cheating father legacy?), I needed someone stable and nurturing. A year after the cranberry juice offering, we were married.

I felt secure and content ...or did I? While Jared wrote his dissertation and held down a taxing teaching gig, I wrote songs and held down a taxing magazine job. Jared did most of the cooking: smoothie breakfasts and baked potato-with-everything-on-it dinners. Potato toppings varied from broccoli and cheddar cheese; to spinach and Feta cheese; to broccoli, spinach, parmesan cheese, and sunflower seeds. Then the cheese was eliminated and the sunflower seeds took center stage. They're full of antioxidants, Jared said, and vitamin E, calcium, iron, zinc. I just want you to be healthy. He worried about my late nights singing at the bar, that I didn't exercise enough or drink enough wheat grass juice. I worried that, hunk though he was, my passion level was the equivalent of sunflower seeds. After four years of marriage, it was over. We cared deeply for each other, but I needed spice.

9. Calamari

Every Friday night I had a date with an older man of few words. What he served up was poetry in a pan: juicy tentacles and rings sautéed in garlic, olive oil and red wine. Chewy, tangy, sensual, every bite forced me to close my eyes and utter a barely audible moan of delight. You like calamari, eh? Joe would ask rhetorically. Joe was the owner and chef (he would call himself a cook) at Little Joe's, the

Columbus Street hangout for locals, students, artists, and financial district types. Friday night was calamari night, and I never missed one. I was on a boyfriend fast after the years of questionable choices and the bittersweet misstep with Jared. So I'd show up at Joe's and sit at the counter. That way I could watch Joe cook. It was like foreplay. All night long he poured the rich olive oil and handfuls of fresh garlic into huge cast iron pans—usually at least four or five going at once—over a high flame. Every few minutes he'd heft one of the pans into the air so that the ingredients got righteously tossed. Occasionally he'd glance over and shoot me a flirtatious half-smile. But it was his food that seduced. The calamari were accompanied by a mound of the most delectable vegetables humankind has ever produced: pan-scalded cauliflower, zucchini, and Italian broccoli flowers, imbued with enough minced garlic to frighten an entire city of hostile vampires. Dinner was served with a tumbler—not a wineglass—of house red. Walking home in the fog I gave silent thanks to Joe, my Friday night ritual, and the tentacled creatures that had found their way into my body.

10. Easter Pie

Mona Lisa looks good in neon, said the stranger with the licorice eyes. His voice was almost subliminal so I couldn't tell if it was his or mine. Allison had dragged me to the opening of the Neon Art Museum downtown insisting my boyfriend fast had lasted long enough and it was time to put myself out there. For art's sake, I said. I turned to the dark-eyed Mona-lover. She glows like no one else, I said. What did you think of the neon cherry pie? he asked. He was still looking at Mona, but shot furtive glances at me with those dreamy eyes. I loved it, I said, especially the swirly-lit cherries. Do you like sweets? he asked.

The following Sunday he picked me up in his vintage turquoise Chevy Bel Air and we drove to east L.A. to sample Mexican pastries. Daniel isn't Mexican – his grandparents emigrated from the knee section of the Italian boot – but he wanted to show me the bakeries on Cesar Chavez Boulevard. So he gallantly opened the door to a new sugar experience: You walk in, grab a metal tray and some tongs, then fill it up with whatever appeals to you from an array of *pan dulce*, Mexican sweet breads in all shapes and fillings: sugar sprinkled, sea shell-shaped *conchas*; sugar-topped croissant-shaped *cuernos de azucar*; *pan de huevo* – sweet egg bread rolls with sugar topping; jelly-filled *empanadas*. We bought some cinnamon-laced Mexican coffee to go with our sweets and stuffed our faces outside the El Gallo Bakery. You've got some sugary lips there, sweetheart, he said. I liked the Bogart voice in his "sweetheart." I liked him. Maybe too much…too soon?

A few days later he invited me to his place to watch "David and Lisa," an old film I had loved as a romantic teenager. When he'd asked about favorite films, I had mentioned this one and he had rented it for us to watch together. I wasn't sure if I'd still feel the same about the characters or be embarrassed to feel an affinity for a film about two teens who fall in love in a mental institution. What I had loved was that the girl only spoke in rhyme. And the boy, averse to touch, finally allows her to get close. Maybe this film was too weird for a second date?

After midnight, in the middle of the film, Daniel asked me to put it on pause for a few minutes. He got up, went into the kitchen and started whisking and mixing. Was he bored with the film? With me? He slid something into the oven and came back to the couch. Kissed me, not for the first time. I could barely focus on the rest of the movie with Daniel's kiss still on my lips, but we watched it as the oven did its thing and a buttery-cinnamon-vanilla scent wafted in from the kitchen. *Look at me, look at me, what do you see, what do you see?* Lisa asked. *I see a girl, a pearl of a girl,* David said, honoring Lisa's rhyming obsession. She's his neon Mona Lisa, Daniel said. Don't move, I'll be right back.

He brought in a spice-fragrant pie topped with pastel-colored sugar sprinkles. What kind of pie? I asked. Easter Pie. My version of an Italian tradition. He cut us each a slice. Creamy ricotta cheese, tangy pineapple bits, soft white rice, cinnamon, vanilla, and another flavor I couldn't identify. It tastes like licorice, I said. It's anisette, he said. I bit into the crust: buttery-sweet and peppery-hot. What's giving it that kick? I asked. White pepper. You like it? Oh yeah.

Easter Pie: hot and sweet, inspired and provocative. What more could I want than a lifetime of fiery sugar?

Several of the stories in this collection were originally published as follows:

"It Will Be Sweet" in *West Magazine, Los Angeles Times*

"Empathy" in *Niche Literary Magazine*

"The First" in *Gold Man Review*

"A Boyfriend History in 10 Flavors" in *Lascaux Review.*

The poem "Angeleno Birch Tree Girl in the Land of Glare" was originally published in *California State Poetry Quarterly.*